FEARLESS AND TRUE®

Wade Bennett

For my mom and dad who brought us from the plains of West Texas to the loveliest Village on the Plains in East Alabama

Dogs, deer, and little children

—1—

He had another bad dream. The bad dreams had come more frequently as he aged, and he sometimes wondered if it was his soul's way of cleansing itself before passing on to the other side. This is where he came in the mornings after having them. He always felt better here in the mornings, bad dreams or not. He was comfortable in this sacred, peaceful place. Beautiful slash pines, magnolias, and white oaks grew here. Many had been felled but the older trees had taken advantage of the space between them and grew mightily. An autumn wind always seemed to sweep gently between the trees. He thought it to be an Auburn wind because even in the heat of the summer, with the shade and breeze, it was cool enough to come here. Lately the city had begun to build an iron fence around the cemetery. He wondered if it was to keep him out. He knew that around town, amongst the socialites, he had developed a reputation as being odd—an easy thing to do in this town, he guessed, but that never bothered him much. Deep down he felt that he had more in common with the men buried here than the ones living in town mingling in the social circles. *Hell, none of them had ever stared down death like these poor boys had*, he thought.

Who were these soldiers, these Texans, was a constant thought for him. If he could just put a few lines together. "Who are these Texans, buried on these plains." A few more lines and he thought he might have something. For quite some time he had been contemplating a poem or short story to explain not just who he really was, but to honor the fallen soldiers buried at his favorite place. Maybe after reading such a story the good townsfolk would understand him a little better. Or maybe he could finally put some peaceful closure on his own experiences. "Who are these Texans" seemed like a nice beginning.

No one seemed to know who they were. They were brought here from The Main on campus to their final resting spot sometime between 1864 and 1865. Some said they died of pneumonia like

Stonewall Jackson had. People seem proud to say that Stonewall died of disease rather than from wounds suffered at the hands of his own men. There was no shame in the painful death by pneumonia and true enough, it had almost killed him, too. Others are said to have died of "fever." With the medical advances since the war he assumed that "fever" would be what the doctors now call "infections." Other soldiers passed from their horrible wounds or worse—from the wounds they caused or saw. He knew firsthand what those horrors could do to a man. Some, simply too tired of living, had nothing left to fight off death any longer. Not many people around town these days could comprehend the horrors of those types of injuries. In his meditations this is where William Paul, retired Colonel of the Confederate States of America, always paused. He would take a deep breath and then say a short prayer to the Father for sparing him a similar fate. He had been razor close to being one of the unnamed soldiers in these graves.

"Who are these Texans, buried on our Auburn plains, ninety-eight gray soldiers, we never knew their names." Wow. He had completed a stanza. How many more would it take? Colonel Paul smiled for a moment before his concentration was broken. Out of the corner of his eye he saw someone approaching. *Dang it, man,* was his first thought. Without even turning his head he knew who was quickly closing in on him. No one, and he meant no one, walked that gingerly, proudly, and earnestly that early in the morning around here. Colonel Paul knew exactly who it was. This morning, a young buck was chasing down this old one, and there was no telling why.

—2—

When he came to within fifty yards, the young buck finally made his presence known, "Hello, Colonel, top of the morning to you." For a moment, the Colonel thought George Petrie would even take off his hat and bow. *He must really want to talk to me*, William thought, but before he could get any words out in return, young George was upon him. The old soldier was a little startled at how quickly he had been closed on in those last thirty yards. *That would have never happened in 1862*, he mused, but that was thirty years ago and here was a young man in his prime.

"Ah, Colonel, I thought I would find you here."

"You mean they told you I was here again."

George flushed with embarrassment. He was a doctor, a scholar, and an honest person who despised gossip. There was no place in a practical world for gossip, he always said. He also could not tell a lie and the redness that enveloped his face told the truth to the Colonel. Fortunately for George, the Colonel had a very soft spot for his young friend and easily let him off the hook. "No worries, young man, what can I do for you this lovely morning?"

Despite the fact that they were having this conversation in the local cemetery, which George found rather odd, instead of in the friendly confines of his university office, the young scholar got straight to the point.

"I need you," he blurted. "I mean," more composed this time, "we need you to help us out this Saturday, William. As you may have heard, my friend, former classmate and counterpart at the University of Georgia, Dr. Charles Herty and I have set up a little match this Saturday, and I would like for you to come along."

"A little match?"

"Yes, a little match known as football," George replied. "And the boys would really like to have you there, Colonel," he added with a smile. William loved that warm smile. *It could break the coldest of hearts*, he thought.

"Well, where will this little match known as football be held, Young Captain?" Young Captain was an affectionate nickname William had given to his young protégé and he only used it when they were in private conversation. The truth is William knew George was a man born after his time—what the old timers called an "old soul." Had they been the same age, it could have been General George Petrie, commanding Army of Northern Virginia or the Potomac standing here instead of "Young Captain."

"Piedmont Park, Atlanta, Georgia," George said proudly.

Atlanta, Georgia, was the last town that William had spent any real time in before landing in East Alabama, and the last time he had ridden a god-awful train. The old soldier despised both Atlanta and trains. There were too many people, too much hustle and bustle, too much noise, and too much traffic to suit him. He had used up his patience for all those things in the war and much preferred the more tranquil, lovely village where he now lived.

"Now George, you know how I feel about trains, and you know how I feel about Atlanta," he began but George was prepared and immediately interrupted, "Listen, that was thirty years ago. God only knows how much I have dreamed about having been there then, but that is all in the past." He continued tenderly, "I sit in on your lectures. You and I founded history here, well mostly you, but I soak it all in and your experiences have shaped me for this moment." He paused. "My moment is finally here to be a field general, not in actual battle but in these new battles, on the field of athletic sports," he continued, "I finally get to feel what it is like to lead men on a field, and I need you there to show me how to do it correctly."

At that moment, William knew he could not resist. He had to gather his thoughts though. After a pause, followed by a deep sigh that seemed to last an eternity to George, William spoke. "You dream of being there and I also dream of being there now, but my dreams are real and brutally painful because I was in the war there. War is not glorious, it is not what you think it is. Sherman was right. It is killing and that's it." Those words stung the young buck, and William knew it, but he continued, "That being said, for you and only you, I will be there."

George could not believe it and stammered in disbelief, "You . . . you will? You mean, you will come with us?"

"Yes, young friend, I will be there. I will return to the place where I almost perished thirty years ago, probably on the same train that brought me here, and I will stand with General George Petrie as he leads his Auburn men onto the field of battle," William said jovially.

General George Petrie. George loved the sound of that. It was one of his fondest daydreams. He was a Virginian, born too late for the Civil War, way too late for the revolution, and the only thing he had ever really attacked were his school textbooks which he mastered with a commander's style. And now, he had this old warhorse going along for this ride.

"Thank you, William. The train leaves Saturday at 6:00 a.m." He shook his old friend's hand and while walking away said a quick prayer to the Father to watch after his buddy. Anyone who hung out with buried soldiers needed looking after. Perhaps Saturday would be a new day for his friend and a successful day for Auburn as well.

—3—

Saturday morning came much quicker for Colonel Paul than he wanted. Since committing to George for his travels, the rest of the week had been a blur. The night before the match, he decided to work in a few whiskey drinks with supper to help him sleep, and it worked. The next morning, he found himself relatively well rested at daybreak, but experiencing an uneasy peace. As he did every morning, he went out onto his porch, drank one cup of coffee, enjoyed his tobacco pipe, and watched the sun rise over the sleepy hamlet. A few minutes passed before his two-year-old tabby arrived with her morning kill to exchange for breakfast. He saw her only two times a day at most—in the morning when he left for the day, and during the evening when he arrived back home. She hunted the bushes around the neighborhood almost the entire rest of the time stalking birds, squirrels, and chipmunks. But her favorite prey was red cardinals. *Goodness, that cat does not like red*, he thought.

For two years now, she was all the company he spent any real time with, other than the buried, unnamed soldiers. For her hunting prowess, Colonel Paul affectionately named her "Tiger." After accepting the morning kills, the Colonel would go inside to prepare her little meal and bring it to her on the porch. He would shake his head and tease her, "Good morning to my own little Auburn Tiger." He would then sit down to finish his pipe before preparing himself for the day.

This morning, he was a bit more prepared than usual. Colonel Paul had laid his clothes out the night before in anticipation of travel. He had also gathered up all the cash money and coins that he had in the house. That came to one ten-dollar gold coin, one ten-dollar greenback, three silver dollars, two dimes and two pennies. In all, twenty-three dollars and twenty-two cents. *You never know what you will need when out on the rail*, he thought.

The morning was colder than normal so on top of his gray wool pants and navy wool shirt, Colonel Paul wore a beige duster and some leather gloves. On the way out the door, he grabbed his old captain's hat from the war, a small flask and several cigars, and caught a glimpse of himself in the mirror. *A real Texas Ranger*, he mused as he grinned and stepped out into the world.

He estimated his walk to the train station would be roughly one-and-a-half miles which would take him past his silent friends at Pine Hill Cemetery. Maybe if he moved at the double-step, he would be able to stop for a few minutes to ask them for some good luck today.

On the way he started thinking about his poem. *Why should I ask, what are your lost names, why do I care, to know your lost fames,* and then he said out loud, "Where are you from, when did you fight, was I with you, did I share your plight?" The second sentence startled him momentarily, and then something happened. At first there was a small shake in his left wrist which slightly curled his left index finger. Then there was a quick wave of nausea, followed by an unexpected light feeling in his stomach. At this point his eyes began to zone in on a target and he marched toward that target with the determination of a train rolling through a tunnel. This old soldier was back in the war and there was little on earth that could stop his momentum.

—4—

The Young Captain had also been up early this morning but unlike Colonel Paul, his night of sleep had not been restful. He had tossed and turned most of the night in anticipation of the next day's match. At one point late the evening before, George went for a brisk twenty-minute walk to calm his nerves, and it worked to some extent. A few blocks from his house he observed a young tabby stalking something in the moonlight under some azalea bushes. *She sure has more confidence in her abilities than I do right now*, George thought to himself. He had been fearless and true all week—until now. Worry, a condition not normally common to him, had begun to set in.

The reality that he had borrowed university money from the local bank to pay for the football uniforms and travels, that all the local dignitaries, their families, and the president of the university—his boss—would be attending the game to witness it all first-hand did not help matters. Not to mention the responsibility of coordinating twelve students, with no telling what they had been up to last night or the condition they would be in this morning, to travel almost three hours to have a match in a relatively new sport against an old friend for the very first time. This had all started to weigh heavily on him. *God knows what awaits us in Atlanta*, he thought. Not to mention, would Colonel Paul show? He really needed him but after speaking with him three days ago, George had not seen him anywhere around campus.

The morning of the game George could not eat. He was dressed and out the door to the train station a good two hours before departure. Once he arrived and saw the train waiting, the workers preparing for departure, and he shook the conductor's hand, his worries began to subside. *If they are ready to roll up those tracks then I must be*, he thought.

After a while, people began to arrive for the trip and at last, the team showed up looking grand. The boys were dressed in navy slacks with beige overcoats and they all wore orange wool caps. George had designed the uniforms with the colors of his alma mater, the University of Virginia, and he thought these young men to be fine Cavaliers. The president of the university, the president of the bank and what seemed to be their entire families had, meanwhile, gathered around George. This was the essence of local politics and George was caught in the middle of the whirlwind of it all. They bombarded him with question after question about today's activities—"What time does the train depart? When will we arrive? How does the game work? What colors will Georgia be wearing? Is this game just a fad? How will the gates be divided?" and on and on. But George, despite earlier doubts about whether or not he could pull this off, handled all of them and their questions with great dexterity. Had he been born sooner, he could just as easily have debated The Articles of Confederation or The Declaration of Independence as flawlessly. If George knew anything, he knew how to connect with people. Despite the doubts that could creep into his confidence while alone, among groups of people he never had any self-doubt.

—5—

The nausea and light stomach were feelings he had not experienced in decades. Not on the day that he had married, or when his children were born, nor even when he buried his wife. It was a feeling he thought had long passed him by—the nervous energy of anticipated death. It was man versus man in the field of battle. Early on in his days as a soldier, the feeling had been so intense he would often vomit, in private if he could, of course, but nonetheless it was always embarrassing even if no one ever mentioned it.

For a moment he thought back to his first battle at Gaines Mill during the Seven Days. He was but a Private at that point and as green as the corn they often ate for supper during his time in the Confederacy. Although part of Hood's Texas Brigade, what General Lee called his "Texas shock troops," he saw little action that day, unlike what was to come. As part of the Ragged 1st, he was mostly in reserve unlike the Bloody 4th and 5th regiments who saw considerable action and gained fame by capturing some New Yorkers' cannons. In fact, the only action he saw was when a confused, wounded Yankee cavalryman wandered into their lines. He and another soldier rushed to capture the poor fellow and his horse but before they could reach him, the man fell over in the saddle, dead. At this sight, the nausea had ended for Colonel Paul but the younger boy with him, an Irishman named Alan, had dropped to his knees and started praying the rosary. That was not the first dead man William Paul had ever seen and it most certainly would not be the last.

About a mile from his current target, Colonel Paul continued to lock onto his objective, the new train depot in town. People were beginning to gather in small crowds. Some were setting up an old telegraph machine on a corner in hopes of updates from Atlanta about the game, while others made their way down to the train. William noticed little of the segregated mobs and continued on a brisk pace to his target. He had learned long ago that when in doubt, focus on a target and begin moving toward it quietly yet forcefully. *It really is amazing how far you can march when you focus*, he thought. Maybe it was the crowd's energy, maybe it was thinking about the Irishman praying from his past, or maybe it was simply from experience, but his nausea subsided. The nervous energy was gone along with the slight spasm in his hand.

For some reason he started thinking about his home in Nacogdoches, Texas, and the small farm where he grew up. He remembered his German mother and Irish/Scottish father, and how hard they had worked. He recalled how his dad had lain dying in bed over a three-day period from sun stroke the July before he left for war, and how his mother had begged him not to go. He would never see her again even though he had promised her he would return. He thought about how far he had come from East Texas through Tennessee, to Virginia and Georgia, just to settle in East Alabama hundreds of miles from a home he now knew he would never see again. He had witnessed and participated in battle in some of the most famously named towns in this country like Gettysburg, Fredericksburg, and Sharpsburg. Now as an older man, he was getting close to boarding a train with a friend to take students from one university to play a match against students from another university in a new sport which he barely knew anything about.

William could not help but feel a little amused. He knew nothing of war until he joined the Confederate Army only to become pretty good at fighting in it. George had tried to explain to him a little of what the sport was all about. William figured at this point he would learn more about it on the train and try to help keep all the dignitaries at bay, perhaps with some anecdotes from the war.

The target was now upon him. Coming from the back of the depot to the front, William was in complete shock at the circus that awaited their departure. "Is the entire town going?" he said aloud to no one. There were people everywhere. Students, faculty, local politicians, families, children, and even some of the local colored townsfolk watched in amazement as the team huddled around George in anticipation of their departure. Several people were obviously already enjoying a drink and swearing loudly about "whipping those Georgia boys." Colonel Paul made his way to the colored crowd who had gathered toward the back of the train. Several of the men there were helping load baggage onto the caboose and the Colonel always felt more comfortable lingering about where work was being accomplished. A few of the men there nodded because they knew him from the cemetery and the Colonel nodded and smiled in return. He recognized them as local grave diggers, and they had the notion that they were not the first grave diggers he had ever seen.

As hard as he tried, William had not escaped the watchful eagle eye of his friend George. Very relieved to see the Colonel, George tipped his hat toward him while the boarding whistle blew and both men stepped onto the train in different cars. William took a deep breath before easing himself up onto a train for the first time since evacuating Atlanta, Georgia, as a wounded rebel. Taking the nearest available seat, he quickly sat down, satisfied that he was not early boarding and not late, but at the right place at the right time as a man should be. *Let's see where this train takes us.*

George had a more difficult time finding a place to sit. Although he was in charge and the captain of this new team, no one had thought to save him a seat. The bankers and their families had boarded and chosen their seats first. Then the president of the university and his party took up almost all of the other seats in first class. With all the orderlies waiting on this car, the cigar smoke billowing from the passengers, plus all their children playing in the aisle, it had become rather stuffy. George navigated as best he could to the back of the car with the hope of finding a spot but was unsuccessful due to some local businessmen enjoying a poker game there. At this point, desperately in need of some fresh air, George moved out of that car and into the next one where the team would be. To his amazement, there was less room here than in the first car. What seemed like several hundred stowaways, other students, had invaded this car. He imagined this is what it must have felt like being transported from battlefield to battlefield in the Civil War. None of this helped his already rattled nerves about the game so George pushed on to the next car. *If this one is full, I guess I'll just go be with the luggage in the caboose*, he thought.

The third car had a more relaxed feel to it with fewer people, much less cigar smoke and no students jumping around. It appeased his sensible mind. In the back of the car, he saw a familiar face tucked beneath a ranger hat and he seemed to be catching a nap. "A nap," he said, "in all this, someone could take a nap?"

George stealthily made his way down the center aisle toward Colonel Paul. About three rows from the seemingly sleeping man, Colonel Paul remarked, "Heck of a racket you got running here, Captain!"

George stopped. "Is there any way I can sneak up on you?"

"I see you in my dreams, George," the Colonel jokingly replied. "Now, Young Captain, what can I do for you?"

"I think I will just sit for a second, that is, if you do not mind some company," George said respectfully.

Colonel Paul made some room and George sat down next to him. The next stop up the rail was the Lee County seat, the city of Opelika. They would stop there momentarily. *Probably to pick up more bankers, lawyers, judges, and dignitaries,* George sarcastically surmised. For a moment they were quiet and the Colonel was just about to begin to nap again when the first question was asked.

"So, do you want to tell me why you do not like trains, William?" George asked.

"Ha, it is a long story, my friend," the Colonel replied. George very rarely called him William and he liked it when he did.

"Well, we have all day, my friend."

Between calling him William and "my friend," Colonel Paul instinctively knew this man needed something to take his mind off his worries. It took him aback. Here was one of the greatest minds in the entire state of Alabama, maybe the entire south, and quite possibly in all of education in this country, and he wanted *his* stories to pass the time. Like most veterans, he listened to stories instead of telling them. Colonel Paul, even in his lectures, never personalized his experiences to the bloody places of which he spoke. His students had an idea of who he was but no one, maybe only his buried wife and those buried Texans in the cemetery, had an inkling of what those old gray eyes had witnessed. So, he took a deep breath, smiled and thought for a second.

"You want to hear about farming in Nacogdoches?" the Colonel teased.

"Well, if that is all you've got, that is all I will take, Colonel Paul," George countered.

Such a simple brilliance you have George, William thought. He really would have sat there for three hours listening to hard scrabble tales of farming in East Texas to pass the time. What anyone else on that train would have thought of as mundane or boring, George would have accepted, enjoyed, and absorbed by the end of the conversation, and most likely would have saved one key piece of the story as information for a later lecture or study. Another trait of being a man, in addition to being on time, Colonel Paul felt, was to make the most of the time God gives you under any circumstances. Nevertheless, farming was not the story he knew George wanted to hear. "I guess I've got something you may be interested in my young friend," he said with a wink, "just to pass the time." And with that Colonel Paul took a cigar out of his pocket, lit the North Carolina tobacco, opened up a small flask of Tennessee whiskey, took a sip and said, "His name was John Bell Hood, and he became my mentor and friend."

Now it was George's turn to smile.

—7—

After leaving his farm in East Texas for war, young William had marched north for a time to the city of Kilgore, Texas. As a young buck, he made the sixty-mile hike in less than three days. For most of the hike, William had been by himself, and he realized this was the farthest he had ever been alone. It was a strange feeling but the longer he walked, the more incredible he began to feel. He was alive and primed for worldly adventures. He was so excited he could barely keep a steady thought on any subject. He had even managed to forget the morbid scene of his father's death about a month earlier. That summer had been a wet one in East Texas and the hillsides were covered with wildflowers of every color. Red, blue, yellow, and white were scattered over the horizon and he could not help but recognize the beauty.

About five miles or so south of Kilgore and the trains that would take him to war, William started encountering small groups of men and boys roughly the same age as he was. They began to march together and the small groups grew bigger and bigger as they approached their destination. William spoke little within the groups but he listened attentively. While working long hours on their small farm, his father would always say, "William, a man listens, learns, and then speaks with confidence." So, he let the groups do the talking while he did the walking and set the pace to their destination. With William at the front of the pack, the group made better time to Kilgore as the march progressed. He was taller, stronger, and could have easily outpaced this group.

"When we got to the station, they packed us in those cars like oysters that are canned for consumption," he said. "It was hot, there was little water, and it would foreshadow the misery that was to come."

Indeed, it was miserable at first. William, trying to make a good impression, was one of the first into his train car and ready to ride. By the time the car had loaded, he had been pushed to the very back with little air left to breathe. Before entering the car, a politician gave a speech to the men and ended it with something about making Texas proud in the war. It was not much of a speech but one thing that William would never forget was the part when the orator asked, "Are you Texans from Sabine, Tyler, or Trinity? Were you raised in Galveston, Harrison, or Gillespie?" How many small towns had all these boys come from and how many small towns across the country were also producing soldiers for this war?

"Somewhere around Shreveport, Louisiana, I had already had enough and while most of the boys started dozing off to sleep due to boredom and the heat, I climbed out of the car, shinnied up the ladder and sat on top of the car for the rest of the ride to Virginia."

"What was it like?" George asked and then jokingly added, "After being in the car up front earlier, I think I know what you mean."

Colonel Paul laughed, "I told you about trains and people, George."

Then Colonel Paul went on to explain how refreshing it was to be on top of that train. It was like being on top of the world. It was like being born all over again. When he looked out over the Louisiana swamps, he visualized Bengal tigers roaming those bayous and hunting down prey. In Jackson, Mississippi, the train stopped and tried to pack in even more future rebels for the ride. By the time the train crossed into Alabama, a few other passengers had figured out his trick and joined him above the heat box below. A young, neglected-looking, curly-haired Irish farm boy named Alan latched onto William. The lad could not have been more than fifteen years old and he looked like he was starving. William had some bread that his mother had packed him for his journey and gave the kid some. The boy had no food but did have some tobacco and they enjoyed a pipe smoke on the train between Montgomery and Atlanta. William had never smoked tobacco before and after coughing the first few pulls of smoke from his lungs, he decided he loved it.

"What was your first impression of Atlanta?" George asked.

"I was too scared to get off the train" Colonel Paul replied. "There were people everywhere and I imagined what it had been like for Spartans to first see the city of Rome."

Young William was indeed too afraid to get off the train, but his new friend Alan was not. It was obvious Alan had survived the world by thievery and hustle. During the small break at the station, Alan had managed to dodge the train guards employed to not allow anyone off, eased himself into the Atlanta market near the train, and quickly made it back to William on top of the train with some fruit, bread, and most importantly, more tobacco. "The kid really was a magician sometimes," Colonel Paul recalled.

By this time, young William had no idea how long they had been on the train or how much longer they would have to ride. Days and nights ran together with stops in big cities and small towns across North Georgia, South Carolina, and North Carolina. Finally, someone came to them and told them they were in Virginia and the last stop was a city called Richmond. "Bet there is lots of tobacco there, William," Alan said with a grin. William laughed but he knew there would be more than tobacco in Richmond. Known on the farm as hard work, there would be war work there and lots of it.

—8—

"When did you meet General Hood?" George asked.

"Patience, Young Captain, I am getting there," Colonel Paul replied.

George had a curious look on his face. Colonel Paul had seen this look when the young buck was in deep concentration. Here was a man who was truly interested in what he had to say. Colonel Paul went to the meat of the story which picked up immediately upon his disembarking the train.

Once they reached Richmond, the men were hurried off the train. On the platform stood one of the most imposing figures William had ever seen. He was not quite as tall as William, but he seemed to hover over everyone. It was their brigade commander, the Kentucky-born but now Texan, John Bell Hood.

"He lined us up quickly, marched us out fast and hard, and took us to the nearest green space available in Richmond."

"What happened next?"

Colonel Paul recanted Hood's words, "You are all Texans of the Texas Brigade. You are part of General Joseph E. Johnston's Army of Northern Virginia. We will march harder than anyone. We will fight harder than anyone. And in the end, there will be nothing but heroes left. TEXANS! MARCH!"

They drilled constantly, slept, drilled more, ate a little, slept, and then one day began a march to the front. Some of them even marched to the front without weapons. William realized very quickly the men without weapons would be able to acquire them from fallen soldiers in battle.

"Just like that, you were in the war?" George asked.

"Yes, just like that. You see, probably like this match today, war is a lot of build up, anticipation, travel, preparation, worrying, waiting and then BOOM, it is on you like a whirlwind and you are right in the middle of it."

"Where did you go first?"

"To the Seven Days against McClellan."

The Colonel went on to explain that he had been selected as a company leader, mainly due to height, but also because of the pace he could set while marching, due to the endurance he built while farming. The little Irishman, young Alan, was still latched right next to him and they, along with about three thousand other men of Hood's Texas Brigade, made their way east of Richmond under the command of Joseph Johnston. This was McClellan's doomed Peninsula Campaign they were fighting in.

"The Seven Days," George said. "Incredible."

"Believe it or not, at first it was quiet for me for the most part. Gaines Mill played hell on the Texas Brigade, but by the luck of the draw or blessings of the Father, I was in reserve or being used as a courier, or on assignment drawing water while aiding the sick."

By this time in the story, Colonel Paul and George had not noticed that the current train they were on had stopped in Opelika, picked up more riders and started back northeast up the tracks toward West Point, Georgia. They had also not noticed several other people gathering around them to listen. Some members of the team, workers on the train, and even a few dignitaries from first class had gathered around the two men.

"Which was luckier, Colonel, you not being killed in your first action, or General Johnston being wounded just enough not to be able to continue his command?" George asked.

By now the questions from George had started to sound like an interview. Colonel Paul was not just passing the time any longer but being debriefed by a master historian. George had begun taking notes on a small pad of paper. The Colonel went on to describe what it was like seeing death. The limbs and other body parts outside the field hospitals had made him vomit—the pools of blood, the screams of horror, the sounds of shells bursting, and the racket from miles away that hundreds of muskets made while firing in unison were all overwhelimng

"Then General Lee took over, and yes, we were both lucky and unlucky that he did."

"How do you mean that?"

"Well, we almost won the war because of his command but the war continued because of it. Had the change of command during the Seven Days not occurred, General Johnston would have continued his retreats, McClellan may have very well marched into Richmond, and the war would have ended sooner at less cost of life. But I would not be sitting here today."

"The fortunes of war," George stated.

Colonel Paul thought about fortunes often. How fortunate you are today from misfortunes that occurred yesterday or vice versa. Life has a way of sneaking up on you, punching you squarely in the face and then completely altering your course. He went on to explain how General Lee completely flipped the tables on the Yankees outside Richmond. In a matter of weeks through pure aggression and audacity, the southerners took all the momentum away from the northerners and drove them from five miles outside their own capital almost into the Atlantic Ocean.

"Never forget, George, it is very important to maintain momentum," Colonel Paul added. "A completely competent commander unleashed his most able subordinates and made them Gods of War on this Earth. Lee was so confident in his abilities and so knowledgeable, it was like he could look into the tent of the other commander's army and anticipate his next move even before they had made a decision."

"When you command . . . command," he went on. "You must make decisions on the best available information possible, make them quickly, and then delegate those choices over to people you have surrounded yourself with that are trustworthy for the task at hand."

George was taking this all in. He had read in his history books of Lee unleashing the likes of Longstreet, Jackson, Hill, and Hood on his enemies, but here was someone who had witnessed it. He was in awe.

"What happened after the Seven Days?"

Colonel Paul smiled and took a small sip of his whiskey. He was about to describe to George some of the greatest times in his life. It was 1862 all over again and part of the greatest years in American History.

"We went on a march, George. We went on a march."

—9—

"Hey, you ol' Texas Aggie, have you told him yet how you met J. B. Hood?" came an unknown voice a few rows up, and was followed by cackling laughter.

Colonel Paul recognized that hyena-like laugh immediately, but it caught George off guard.

"Excuse me, sir?" George replied rather aggressively.

"I said, this Texas farm boy needs to explain his introduction to the great General Hood, sir," which was again followed with that menacing heckle of a laugh.

"George," Colonel Paul said while shaking his head, "do you know Doc Greene?"

George stood up and composed himself, "No, I am afraid we have not been introduced."

William grinned and thought to himself that this should be interesting. Doctor Walter Greene must have hopped the train in Opelika while the two of them were in deep discussion. He was an old acquaintance of Colonel Paul's who had moved his practice from Auburn to Opelika a few years back. The good doctor was raised in this area by his father, a doctor from Atlanta who had served in the Civil War. His father's nurse was an Indian woman who traced her heritage to the local Creek Indian tribe. Doctor Greene, the senior, was on the same train that evacuated William Paul and several hundred other Texas soldiers from Atlanta before it fell. Also on that train was the doctor's daughter, also a nurse, whom William would one day marry. And the pride of the family, Doc senior's baby boy Walter Greene, now stood here heckling his old brother-in-law.

"I heard from the poker game that there was a burly old veteran in the back car, and somehow knew that Colonel William Paul, Confederate States of America, would be on this voyage," Doc Greene said.

"And you thought that this Colonel may or may not have a sip of whiskey for an old friend, perhaps?"

"Well, they would not let me join their poker game up there after what happened last time, so perhaps, an old friend may have a nip for an old friend, yes," Doc Greene retorted.

What happened the last time Doc Greene played poker is the stuff of local legend. He may or may not have cleaned out half the town including the local judge, police chief, and several other important people around Auburn. The rumor was that he had even won the deed to half of downtown. Afterwards, and probably involving some sober reflection, the good doctor moved his practice up the road to Opelika and had not set foot in Auburn since.

Colonel Paul passed the flask to his former family member, made formal introductions between George and their new audience member, and then settled back into his story.

"Now, George, where were we?" he said. "Oh yes, before our interruption, we had just witnessed history when General Lee took over for General Johnston. The Texans, along with the rest of the CSA in the east, had pushed McClellan back to the safety of his gunboats near the Atlantic, and then we started to move toward the next phase of the war on the plains of Manassas."

The present day train pulled into the depot in West Point, Georgia. There would be a short break but most of the people in their car stayed to listen attentively to Colonel Paul. He explained that after pushing the Yankees away from Richmond, General Lee wanted to relieve even more pressure for his home state. Lee motioned Stonewall Jackson to move into the Shenandoah Valley. This was always one of Lee's classic moves when he needed to confuse and startle the northern command in Washington. By the time Stonewall took off for the Valley, President Lincoln and his advisors had decided that McClellan's effort east of Richmond would fail, and they began withdrawing troops from there to Northern Virginia under a new Yankee commander, General Pope.

"The miscreant?" George asked.

"Yes, the bloody miscreant bastard!" Doc Greene piped in harshly.

"Doc, let's have one storyteller at a time now," Colonel Paul said jokingly.

"Well, the truth is the truth. What a bloody man he was," Greene said.

George blushed at the language, but the truth *was* the truth. As a young man, Doc Greene had heard all the old war stories from his field surgeon father. Then, as he grew in age and began to know Colonel Paul, he heard at family dinners and holiday gatherings all the rest he had wanted to hear about those days. If ever there was any Yankee General who brought out the wrath of southern men, besides William Tecumseh Sherman, it was General Pope with all his bluster. A southern man will not stand for there being too much tail to a kite.

Colonel Paul went on to explain that Lee, even before his counterpart could, quickly realized that McClellan's forces were to be withdrawn. The only decision then was to move his forces away from Richmond and into Northern Virginia to confront the miscreant before he was at full strength. With Stonewall almost already in the Valley, the objective would be the Orange and Alexandria Railroad near the Battle of First Bull Run on the plains of Manassas somewhere behind Pope's line of supply.

"By the time we got into motion to join Jackson, our Texas Brigade had been fairly decimated at Gaines Mill. We lost the majority of our officer core when the 4th and 5th stopped a counter attack and then proceeded to charge some New Yorkers' cannons."

"Were they Zouaves?" George asked. It was like he was piecing together the entire part of that battle in his mind for a future lecture.

"No, they would come later."

At this point, Colonel Paul explained how he became an officer. There were so few left alive after the Seven Days, that the men were ordered to elect two from every regiment to supplement the pool. Later in the war, Texans would insist they elected their officers no matter the rank, if possible. William was elected mainly on his physical ability to march without exhaustion. In a matter of months, the fortunes of war had taken this "Texas Aggie" from an innocent young farm boy to a lieutenant in the army of Northern Virginia.

—10—

George had been taking notes from Colonel Paul all right, but not the type that Colonel Paul probably thought he was taking. The Young Captain was leading his own army into battle today for the first time. He was beyond excited and attempting to put into words what the day meant. The Colonel talked of marching and war, but also about the meaning of friendship, duty, and hard work. When put together in times of stress, what groups of people could accomplish was stunning. Groups of people from all over the country, without any knowledge of one another beforehand, could suddenly rally together to achieve the unachievable. It was remarkable to him that a young boy from a remote place could so rapidly rise to lead other young men from even more remote places into battle. "God's ways truly are not our ways," he wrote on his pad.

"So, how did you finally meet General Hood?" George asked.

With this prompting, Colonel Paul began to describe his experience at the Battle of 2nd Manassas. With a wide left flanking maneuver, Stonewall Jackson and his troops had marched fifty miles into General Pope's rear to wreck his supply depot. When the Yankee general realized that the southern forces had split into two wings, he began a rear motion to attack Jackson and destroy the rebels by piecemeal. Colonel Paul shared how he, along with the rest of General Longstreet's corps, made almost the exact same march as Jackson's boys at the exact same time they did to reunite the army.

"By the time we caught up with Jackson, he was in one hell of a fight," Colonel Paul added.

Jackson was indeed in a fight and had been for some time. His boys were dug into an old railroad cut that served as a ready-made defense trench. Pope had been coming at Stonewall for two days with blue wave after blue wave of Union soldiers to no avail. *As much of a miscreant as he was considered,* George thought, *it sure sounds like Pope was not afraid to fight.*

"Stonewall was just about to break, but Longstreet slipped us into the right of the railroad cut without Pope noticing at the exact right time, and then we opened up on the Union flank."

The Texans were positioned directly next to Stonewall Jackson's right flank and formed like a hinge on a door to the left flank of Longstreet. "We were perched with some South Carolina artillery on a knoll concealed by a tree line, and had a bird's eye view of the feast coming to us." That feast was Porter's men and the South Carolina artillery opened up their cannons first. "It stopped the Yankees dead in their tracks."

"Then what happened?" George asked.

"We instinctively charged. The artillery barrage completely buckled the Union advance. When the Texans started to charge, they let out a yell that sounded like a pack of a thousand coyotes howling during the chase of their next meal. Longstreet's entire left flank crashed into the startled blue soldiers and swept them off the field of battle. This is when we hit the Zouaves, George" Colonel Paul said emphatically.

The listening crowd heard the story about those New Yorkers. Hood's Texas boys had already had some encounters with the New Yorkers and did not care for them one bit. For one thing, they dressed strangely, they talked strangely, and back around Richmond, the two groups of men had shared rival picket lines and had words. "They were arrogant as hell," he said of the New Yorkers, "and we wanted a piece of them pretty badly."

What Colonel Paul explained about getting a "piece of them" sounded to George like straight murder and rage from both sides. "To their credit," the Colonel allowed, "those New York boys held their own for as long as possible and probably saved us Texans from running to the gates of Washington itself."

The Colonel described the killings—how he had shot a man from New York between the eyes from two feet away, and the sound that a rifle butt makes when it crushes a skull. He related what it felt like to stab someone to death, and the shocking amount of blood large groups of men lose when fighting amongst each other to the death. He told what it was like to be hit, stabbed, kicked, bitten, shot, and to survive. But the worst feeling of all is when it is all over and that eerie silence washes over the battlefield and the dead.

"Those poor Zouaves," he said, "with all their funny uniforms and colors. They were scattered over a hillside, dead. All the blue, yellow, red, and white . . . it reminded me of that time on the Texas countryside when I was marching to Kilgore and saw all those wildflowers after a cool summer rain, and it made me sick for home."

—11—

"Colonel, would you like to take a break?" George offered.

"Yes, perhaps we should save some of these stories for further down the rail," added Doc Greene.

During the storytelling session, Doc Greene had begun to ease closer to where both George and Colonel Paul had been sitting. For all his quirks and jesting ways, he was very keen and observant toward people. The Doc first noticed the slight twitch in Colonel Paul's left hand when he began to tell the story of 2nd Manassas. Then there was the shallow breathing, what appeared to be sweat building up underneath his hat line, and the natural color of the man's skin turning to a lighter shade of pale. Had he been closer to observe the Colonel, he would have noticed the dilated pupils that accompanied a rapid increase in the patient's heartbeat.

George had noticed this as well. He could not pinpoint exactly what the symptoms were with Colonel Paul, but it was like there had been a decrease in barometric pressure within the cabin of the train. He was afraid to look at the Colonel and kept his head down while pretending to take some more notes. *Was I sitting next to a ghost?* he wondered.

Taking a deep breath, Colonel Paul said, "I'm fine," but he was not fine, and his two friends knew it.

Doc Greene discreetly motioned for an orderly and asked him to quickly bring some water, a few clean towels, and some more whiskey if he could find it—but, the water and towels first.

"He came up on horseback behind me in the aftermath, and said, 'Lieutenant, see to your men!'"

"Who did, Colonel?" George asked.

It was General Hood who spoke as he stood in front of the mounds of dead New York soldiers, Texans, and South Carolinians. General Hood had noticed a strange figure towering over the carnage. He had immediately come to investigate only to find young William Paul blood-soaked and stunned, calmly observing the sight.

"Lieutenant," he shouted, "See to your men!"

"Lieutenant!" General Hood yelled again.

This time William Paul turned to answer. "Yes, sir!"

As he turned, General Hood immediately noticed the young officer's face was covered with dirt and blood. He became flush with sympathy and said, "Son, I know what you are thinking, but we have many hard days, work, and battles before we can get back home."

"Yes, sir, General," William responded.

"You fought very well today, young man, and your General is pleased with you and all of his Texans. Now, you must see to your men who are still with us."

"Thank you, sir," William said and as he saluted and turned away to find his men, he heard, "No, thank you, son," from General Hood.

At this, William made his way to a commotion of men and horses almost forty yards to his front. On the downslope of a small hill, he found Alan still alive and in the process of trying to requisition two wagons previously owned by the New York battery they had just defeated. Several South Carolina boys from Wade Hampton's brigade were also trying to requisition the wagons and a small scuffle had broken out between them and Alan. In no mood to fight with anyone, William approached the group with his sword in one hand and his empty revolver in the other.

"You men scatter this area immediately," William said.

"I think you should be the ones leaving the area, Lieutenant," snapped one of the South Carolina boys. He was a Captain who outranked William.

"At that, I put the sword to his neck and the pistol to his head and said, 'Then we shall all stay here.'"

At that moment, several large groups of soldiers, officers, cooks, and grave diggers gathered around the wagons.

"All that for some wagons?"

"You see, George, war is pure consumption. It consumes everything and makes what is left more valuable than in normal times. A rock, a creek, a hillside, a tree to hide behind all become vitally important to survival. So, something of military value that is actually left in working order after a battle, or even better, food, is sought after at the highest premium."

What Colonel Paul knew from experience was that in war, the value of anything increases a hundred times over that same object in peacetime. Those wagons could help the Texans haul their wounded to the hospital the same as they could help the South Carolina boys haul their wounded to their hospitals. One wagon, one horse, one extra meal, one extra cartridge, one more hillside held or road taken could win the war.

"That's crazy," Doc Greene said.

"Yes, and just before I got around to stabbing some poor South Carolina fellow in the neck over a wagon, General Hood showed up. The General ordered the fighting to stop and commandeered with rank the wagons for The Texas Brigade. But that was not the end of it."

"What then?"

Colonel Paul continued, "It seems a few of the South Carolina boys were still upset, so about an hour later, General Shanks showed up in the camp to discuss the matter with General Hood. Shanks was from South Carolina and although under no authority to our brigade, had accompanied General Hood into Manassas with zero authority but a higher rank. That old Gamecock demanded those wagons back," he cackled. "Can you believe that?"

"Unbelievable," George remarked while shaking his head in disbelief.

The story took an even more morbid turn when the "old Gamecock" also requested the hide of the man who threatened to stab one of his soldiers in the throat over the wagon.

"Now General Hood was having none of any of this, especially the request for my hide," Colonel Paul said. That was one thing people admired most about General Hood. He was the bravest human they knew. He also had their back covered no matter what, and in return they charged hell for him. A man has his friends back, even when they are wrong.

"So, Colonel, who ended up with the wagons?" asked George.

"Well, of course, South Carolina did. Longstreet settled the matter."

"James Peter Longstreet," Doc Greene said wryly.

"Yes, Lee's old war horse himself stepped in," William said with a smirk.

The truth is it had been no laughing matter. Both General Hood and General Shanks were fighting mad about the incident and the current dustup was quickly escalating into another brawl between the two. Longstreet, who outranked just about everyone on earth other than General Lee, had caught wind of the tension. He was none too happy to have to settle what he thought of as such a petty thing as a few wagons with so much work left to do after the victory.

"Longstreet had the utmost patience in battle but between people, he could be down-right rude. The exchange went like this . . . "

"Get these damn wagons out of here and where they belong, General Hood!" General Longstreet yelled.

"They belong with me," General Hood replied.

"I am ordering you to release those wagons over to General Shanks immediately," General Longstreet countered and then added, "with an apology, sir."

"Fine. But let me get my dead off of them first," General Hood snarled. "But General Shanks and that apology can go straight to hell, sir," and then as if finishing a play, Hood took his hat off and bowed to General Longstreet.

"Consider yourself under arrest," Longstreet said sternly.

"Good grief, he arrested him?" Doc Greene asked.

"Yes and no. He was allowed to travel with the brigade until a formal court martial could take place."

"Seems harsh, but he was insubordinate to not one but two commanding officers," George added.

At this Colonel Paul started laughing hysterically. "George, I never knew you to be such a stick-in-the-mud rule follower," he teased.

The truth is George Petrie had never been a teetotaler, he had simply always done everything in his entire life correctly.

"Yeah, how about a sip of this fine whiskey, you ol' rebel?" Doc Greene nodded to George.

In a full blush and to deflect the joking, George quickly tried to refocus the discussion. "Please continue with the story Colonel."

'Well, that is about it, I suppose," said Colonel Paul.

"That cannot be it!" George said incredulously.

"Hood was escorted to his tent," the Colonel continued. "But before he retired, he called on me, looked me square in the eyes, smiled than ordered, 'Young Captain, see to those wounded and then turn the wagons over to those people,' as he pointed at the South Carolinians."

"And that is how you became a Captain? With a battlefield commission from General Hood over a wagon fight?"

"Yes, George, that is how I became Hood's "Young Captain," for having my friend's back, and now you know why I call you that," Colonel Paul grinned.

—12—

George needed a break. The train was quickly approaching LaGrange, Georgia, and would be stopping for a few minutes. He could tell Doc Greene was equally concerned about the Colonel and he wanted to politely give the doctor a few minutes to observe the man close up.

George excused himself saying he needed to check on the team and swiftly moved to the front of the car. An orderly rushing through the aisle almost spilled a pitcher of cold water all over him. Frustrated, he stopped for a second to give the helper a glare of disapproval, but his anger subsided quickly when he noticed the orderly giving Doc Greene the water with a few towels that would be used to cool Colonel Paul down.

George proceeded to make his way into the car with the team. Several of the boys were reviewing some notes that George had cataloged together for them about the match later today. There were pages in small books containing formations, scenarios, and how the boys would line up on both offense and defense according to the time and place of the game. George had named several pages "plays" like they were certain acts in a script. But he knew these boys would be actors in a much different way today, although George did ponder the similarities in theatre and this new athletic event. The field was a stage which would have spectators. There would be an opening, several "acts," an intermission, and then action would resume unfolding to an ending. Hopefully, the ending would not be too dramatic and would result in his boys as victors.

Inside the car were Wallace, Lupton, Gaston, Dorsey, Murphy, and Wright. They were older students and had gathered in the back of the car to review a few plays. Wright was one of George's favorites. He was a hazel-eyed, brown-haired young man with a quiet but fully determined disposition. Wright had a welcoming, honest face and George had decided to name him today's player captain before the game. The truth was Wright reminded George of himself as a younger man because this young man was also mastering his studies off the field in the classroom, which to George was as important as anything else.

"How are we, men?" George addressed the group.

"Good, great, sir. Just reviewing some notes before the game while we can." They all looked eagerly at him.

Good, George thought, *making the most of their time while they can*. He squatted down in the aisle near the boys and started to review some plays with them. During the discussion, he quizzed the group about certain scenarios and possible outcomes during certain times of the game. George preached new concepts to his team such as down and distance, sound defense, maintaining momentum and pace, staying loose but paying strict attention to details. Other players gathered around the group and a full on pre-game meeting was suddenly underway. There was an intense conversation between coach and players. George made some adjustments to a few plays and even added what he called an "end around" to play number three in the book which he renamed "Manassas." The idea for the play came to him earlier while listening to Colonel Paul.

"You see men, we are going to pound on their lines all day and when they are tired or least expect it, we will out flank them with this adjustment called "Manassas," the coach explained proudly.

The boys were thrilled. George could tell they were ready. For a few weeks now, they had drilled, practiced, drilled more, exercised and worked as hard as humanly possible in between their schoolwork and sleep. They had grown tired of tackling one another and hungered for a chance to battle someone else. George was also hungry to see how well not only they, but he, matched up with his old counterpart on the football field of battle.

George had not even noticed the train pulling into the station in LaGrange and then starting back up for Atlanta. There would be just a few more stops before entering the great city and then a few more stops after that before Piedmont Park. Unlike the Colonel in the back of the train, George loved Atlanta and thought of the city as a great one. He likened the city to a bright new star in a bright new south. He had momentarily forgotten about the Colonel and was in private conversation with Wright about being a team captain and what he thought it meant to be a leader. George had wanted to discuss with the young man his new status before he disclosed his decision to the rest of the team.

Some time had passed when a young colored man who had helped with the baggage came into the team car in a frantic search for George.

"D-d-doctor Petrie," he stammered out forcefully. "They sent me here to get you. Come quick."

This not only startled George but the entire team. The young man had a very forceful way about him but a very nervous, scared look on his face. Immediately George rose to follow him and the entire team starting with Wright lined up to follow.

"Is everything okay, son?" George asked the young man.

"Don't know," he responded. "Doc Greene said get you so I came and got you."

Worried, George thanked the young man and then proceeded with his team into the back car, having no idea what awaited them.

—13—

Quite shaken, George entered the Colonel's car. He was concerned and had not liked the look in the young man's eyes that came to fetch him. That had been honest fear and he knew it. In the few seconds it took George to walk back to the car, thousands of negative thoughts raced through his mind such as: *What if I pushed the Colonel too far? What if there is an emergency and we have to stop? Will we even make it to Atlanta?* To his relief, the scene in the back of the train was not one of panic and Doc Greene clearly was in control of whatever had occurred.

The Colonel had been placed horizontally on a seat that was now a makeshift bed. Doc Greene had his stethoscope on and was carefully listening. A few of the orderlies were helping Doc, including their foreman, whom everyone around town called "Buck." They had hopped on the train to help with the luggage and equipment for the game. Buck squatted down at one end of the seat, applying some slight pressure to the Colonel's neck to stabilize him, and was slowly patting the top of the Colonel's head and the back of his neck with a damp towel. A few windows had been opened to move some fresh air through the car.

"Doc, what happened?" exclaimed George. "Is he going to be okay?"

"He is dying, George," Doc replied without stopping his examination. "Not today, but soon."

The entire car, including several of the players who had rushed back to see what was happening, fell silent. Only the sounds of the train reverberating on the tracks, the wind whistling through the windows, and Buck whispering a prayer into the Colonel's ear could be heard.

"Should we stop now and get him to a hospital?" George asked.

"His heart is fine and in fact, it's as strong as a young buck's," Doc said.

"Then, what happened Doc?"

"Buck, you keep him still now, keep that water on him, and stay right here with him, you hear?" Doc ordered.

"Yes sir," Buck responded before returning to his mumbled prayers.

Doc Greene then turned to George as he took his stethoscope off and motioned for him to walk with him to the front of the car. George knew Doc was worried but calm.

"Coach, the Colonel has seen and committed a lot of violence in his life. My father, who attended to these men in the war, told me what it was like for the survivors. They may have lived through the horrors, but parts of them died. The rest of the body goes on, and becomes even stronger to compensate. But, over time, the part of the body that died begins to take over. Do you understand?"

George took a deep breath and honestly replied that he did not understand.

Doc patiently explained, "You see, this is about the soul. The non-scientific part of life that only God understands. George, all the experiences you, I, the Colonel, and everyone has in life leaves an imprint on our souls. When you are young, strong, and tough as nails, your body compensates for anything bad that you have seen or experienced. The Colonel has seen more trauma in his life than anyone I know, except for my father who treated men like him. Now that the Colonel is up in age, is more alone, and has the time to reflect on his life, his body cannot cover for his soul any longer. The imprints, or memories as we may call them, are beginning to regurgitate from his spirit."

George, always observing and learning, someone who excelled in all things Science and History, was a little stumped here. He had no experience with trauma like this. His life had been one of wonder, exploration, learning, and looking toward the future. Life was always something new to him—like today's game against Georgia, a new concept of competition. Although he believed in God, and practiced religion, hearing a doctor who made calculated scientific decisions discuss the concept of a soul ailing so much that it could end a life was baffling.

"Doc, what do we need to do?" George puzzled.

Doc knew that the Colonel was in some type of soldier shock. Minutes before collapsing, Colonel Paul had been staring off in the distance out the windows of the train at the fallow and harvested sweet cornfields of middle Georgia. Doc knew that the Colonel's thoughts were somewhere else in some distant time and place. The cornfield had set the entire episode in motion.

"George, let's get him stable and maybe we should stop the discussion of the war for the rest of the ride to Atlanta," Doc diagnosed.

At that moment Buck interrupted the conversation between the two men with, "He is awake and up."

Both Doc Greene and George immediately went to the Colonel who by now was surrounded by what seemed to be half of the train's passengers.

"Young Captain, you look as though you have seen a ghost," Colonel Paul said with a sheepish grin.

Somewhat relieved, George replied, "I think I may have."

"Buck, what the hell are you doing back here?" the Colonel said jokingly.

With a big beautiful smile, Buck replied, "Telling them haints to get off you, Colonel. You need to stay out of that cemetery talking to them. You gonna have plenty of time to rest there one day. Ain't no use in calling them up to come get you early!"

With a snort, Colonel Paul said, "You are right Buck, you are right." The Colonel knew Buck very well from spending time talking to his Texans in the cemetery. Over the years, he had watched Buck and his crew dig the graves for several Auburn men, women, and children. This included the grave for his deceased wife. Buck also knew something about death, and that common bond formed a mutual respect between the two men.

As everyone stared at Colonel Paul, he took his flask from his pocket, opened the top, took a small nip and passed it to Buck who in turn took a drink, and passed it to the next man. Doc Greene was not drinking, still in full observation mode of his patient. Neither was George, so he politely passed the flask to the next man.

"Doc, I guess I had another one of my bad dreams," Colonel Paul sighed.

"The cornfields triggered it, Colonel," Doc offered.

"Ah, the broken cornfields," the Colonel said. Reaching into his pocket, he pulled out the three silver dollars he had stashed earlier back in Auburn and handed them to Buck. He asked Buck to make his way to the front of the train, pay for some more liquor to fill his flask, and then bring it back to him.

"Keep any of the change, Buck," Colonel Paul said. He then winked at the muscular Negro and said, "It seems I may not be needing it much longer."

At this George stepped in to command, "Okay, everyone. Let's give Colonel Paul some room to breathe."

The crowded train car began to disperse leaving Colonel Paul, Doc Greene, George and a few of the team players behind. A slight chill had set in due to the windows being open. Doc Greene asked some of the players to close them. While they obliged, Colonel Paul asked George if he wanted to hear about the cornfields.

Doc Greene immediately interrupted, "Maybe we should talk about something else for now, Colonel."

Colonel Paul gave Doc Greene a stubborn look and said, "I will discuss what I damn well want to and have to, Doc." And with that, George sat back down next to the Colonel and took his notepad out to record what was said.

—14—

"Other than the Devil's Den at Gettysburg, I have never seen such slaughter," Colonel Paul began.

Doc Greene tried to intervene again but Colonel Paul would have none of it. He now *needed* to tell his story. While he was enveloped in his "bad dream" from moments ago, he vividly relived those terrifying moments of his life. He went on to tell George, Doc Greene, and now a few of the football teammates who were listening, about Antietam.

After whipping Pope's Federal Army at Second Manassas, he as a Captain in Hood's Texas Brigade, along with roughly forty thousand other hungry wolves in the Confederate Army, crossed over the Potomac River and invaded the great state of Maryland. Their goal, according to the Colonel, was Harrisburg, Pennsylvania. The army was to quickly move there, destroy a vital bridge over the Susquehanna River connecting that state to the rest of the north, then march on and destroy Baltimore while a startled Yankee Army watched in disbelief.

"At that point, without a Yankee intervention, the war would have been practically over," Colonel Paul explained.

George was stunned. *The war would have been over? An actual victory was a real possibility for the confederacy?* In today's world, this new world and South, thirty years after the end of the Civil War, it was very difficult for this thinker to ponder that possibility. There was nothing that made sense about that scenario to such a practical man. George loved his country. He loved the United States which, in his opinion, was the most absolute land of possibility ever created. And now sitting next to him this man, of age and experience, was telling him confidently how close the country was just thirty years ago to not existing. That would have to be a possibility for reflection that George would need to save for another day.

Buck reappeared with a flask of brandy that he had procured in exchange for one silver dollar. He handed the flask to Colonel Paul and tried to give the other two silver dollars back to him.

George noticed and appreciated the honesty and truthfulness of the man. He thought those to be the most respectful attributes in the human creation. Colonel Paul refused the money and at that Buck said, "I ain't taking no money from no dead man walking."

"Buck, he's not dead yet!" Doc observed.

For all the crazy stories George had heard about Dr. Walter Greene, he was sure to catalog the human touch he displayed with this patient. There was a certain sympathy in the man. This was another attribute of the human experience that George appreciated.

"I guess I'll keep one dollar and split the other dollar with the other two men helping," Buck stated.

It was obvious Buck cared for his people and loved them. George admired Buck's humility.

Colonel Paul opened the flask, took a drink and then offered some to Doc Greene. "Not yet, Colonel, I am still working," the Doctor declined. The Colonel started back up explaining the current situation of the South's invasion of the North.

"By this time, George McClellan had replaced General Pope and was back for a second go around at the head of the Army of the Potomac. The Northern Army was not surprised at all. In fact, McClellan had rallied his Army and they were also on the march. Not only that, the Confederate Army was greatly outnumbered two to one. The Yankees were moving in mass hard and fast through the west Maryland mountains to intercept us. McClellan was was on to us."

Still taking notes, George inquired, "What happened next?"

"We were spread out, tired and nearly starving. By this point in the invasion, the army of the south was spread out in western Maryland from Harper's Ferry, Virginia to Hagerstown, Maryland. Many of the men did not even have shoes. West of the Catoctin Mountains lay a small hamlet called Sharpsburg. The Colonel was with Longstreet north of the town in Hagerstown. When the enemy's plan revealed itself, they were ordered to counter back to Sharpsburg where General Lee would consolidate his army to absorb the now certain battle with the entire Army of The Potomac. Even for hard marchers like the Texans, it was exhausting. I was now just north of the town of Sharpsburg, positioned with General Hood and the men behind old Dunker Church trying to find something to eat."

"General Hood was there and not still under arrest?"

"Very good, Young Captain, you were listening earlier," Colonel Paul joked. "Indeed, he was back leading again, and we could not have been happier. On the march, some of the boys appealed to General Lee for his return. The good General knowingly obliged what kind of work we could do with Hood at the front."

George knew from his studies and listening to this veteran just what kind of work General Lee always had in mind for the Texans. Those Texans were Lee's murder of crows, and they would be called on time and again for absolute shock and killing in mass. The Colonel described what transpired next.

"The Rebels were still very fragmented in formation with a powerful and consolidated force about to bear down on their position. While cooking breakfast on that mid-September morning, before the boys could finally have something to eat, the Yankees struck. General Hooker and his men had pushed Rebel pickets out of a cornfield in front of the church and they were threatening to roll up the entire left flank of the Confederate Army. This time it would not be Longstreet or even Lee to call on the Texans for help. It would be Stonewall Jackson asking for aid."

"Old Blue Light?"

"Yes, the one and only. Longstreet had moved his men to the south of the church and Hood was in reserve behind the flank of Stonewall who was to the North. Again, the Texans seemed to be the hinge between the two wings of Lee's armies of Jackson and Longstreet.

"Sort of like the clavicle connecting the right and left shoulders," Doc blurted out with a twinkle in his eye.

The two men listened on as Colonel Paul described the carnage of the cornfield. Hooker had pressed Jackson's men through the field and into some woods near the church. Stonewall and his men had almost broken when the fury of the hungry Texans was unleashed on Hooker. "You do not know anger until you experience it coupled with true hunger. Imagine yourself frying what little food of bacon grease and flour you have while starving, then being interrupted by people trying to kill you before you can have a bite to eat. Our response was rude to General Hooker's interruption. The furious Texans went in with close to twenty-five hundred men. By the time they were finished, the cornfield was fallow and so was Hooker's attack."

George listened in horror as Colonel Paul described what killing men was like that day. The Southerners drove the Yankees back from the woods, out of the cornfields and back to the safety behind their artillery. Had there been more men to follow up the Texan counterpunch, it would have been Lee rolling up the Northern flank that day instead of the Yankees almost rolling up the Southern one. All because of the Texas shock troops.

"Of all the things that happened that day, two things stood out more than anything to me. A hungry man is capable of anything. They will kill, steal, fight, hurt, stab, murder, and rob just for a piece of bacon." Colonel Paul said.

"What else stood out?" inquired George.

"Every time I see a harvested corn field, I return to that day. We left nothing and everything in that Maryland field. After we were finished, there was not a blade of corn left growing. That place was broken forever and those of us fortunate enough to survive were as well," said a solemn Colonel Paul.

—15—

As the stories from the back of the train car flowed like the sweet brandy from the Colonel's flask, no one noticed the train come into the next station, stop, and then continue its movement northeast toward Atlanta. The weather for most of the morning had been dreadful. It was a gloomy February morning in the South. Cold, wet, and windy, with low clouds offering more than a hint of bad weather. The outside panorama was rather depressing. For the passengers, the old war stories at first had been exciting and entertaining, but as the train rolled up the rail, the stories became more harsh and the reality of the war unfolded into complete brutality. The ride to Atlanta was now more a test of endurance with what waited at the end of the line still a complete mystery. Much like the thousands of young and eager men who entered the American Civil War, no one on board quite knew what to expect later on, and the trip had already taken several unusual twists and turns.

For a few miles, everyone sat in silence. The train would be in Newnan, Georgia, at the next stop. That was considered the halfway point. There would be a break in the ride for the train to take on water and supplies. The passengers could disembark, stretch and take a few minutes to refresh themselves. The next stop after Newnan would be Union City which was just outside the southwestern part of Atlanta. George had always thought the name quite ironic when passing through during his travels. Seeing as how it was Union troops that burned Atlanta to the ground, this smaller city sat at this side of the big city as the entry point. After that, the train would move into Atlanta, directly to Piedmont Park, and to one of the South's first football matches between two universities.

Just outside Newnan, Colonel Paul was the first to notice the sun beginning to peek through the winter clouds and light rain.

"It really is beautiful," the Colonel proclaimed.

"What is?" asked a startled George. He was glad to hear the voice of his friend. He had been very worried after the earlier episode with the Colonel.

"The sun, George. The rays peeking through the clouds."

"Are you okay, Colonel?"

"I was in Fredericksburg, Virginia, once, George. The Yankees had beaten us pretty good back into Virginia from Maryland. I was sitting on top of a hill outside Fredericksburg one morning, cold and hungry. We had taken a very strong defensive position overlooking the city on the opposite side of the river. Our troops were cut into the hill behind a stone wall on what is now called Marye's Heights. Our line crisscrossed for a few miles according to the natural defensive topography."

George knew this terrain well having studied this battle when he was younger. General James Longstreet had devised a defensive network that the Union Army would unfortunately find out was impregnable.

"As usual, Texans were the hinge between the two corps of Lee's army. Thankfully, this time, we were acting more as reserve than anything. To the left of us sprawling down the heights was Longstreet and to the right, their lines moving like a snake down river, was Stonewall."

"That sounds like about as safe a place as you can be in a battle line, Colonel."

Colonel Paul thought about that for a second and responded, "You know, generally it was the worst place to be in between those two killers, but this time it actually *was* the safest place." And with a wink he added, "I guess that is why I actually had time to enjoy the view."

The Colonel was enjoying the view. He was back in Virginia and the sun was peeking through the clouds on a cold December morning. By this time in the war, just a year into it, he had been promoted to Major and served more as a liaison on staff for General Hood. Staff work was generally considered a little less dangerous except that he was with Hood who was always in the middle of the fight. Hood, at this time, would receive orders from Lee or Longstreet, and then his staff would see that those orders were carried out by the officers in charge of the troops.

"Fredericksburg just seems like it was so unnecessary, Colonel."

"The whole war was unnecessary, George. It was just another murderous blunder along the waste that the entire thing was!"

George really did not know how to react to that. Like most men his age, he had heard all the stories of the war, but unlike many of the men his age, he had thoroughly studied its events. He had never really contemplated the necessity of it all. For him it was something, although obviously unfortunate in many aspects, that needed to be studied for better understanding. This ride had turned into one of his greatest studies because here was an actual oral history lesson with raw fact and no romantic notions of the subject matter. It was both history and science. Like much science, the actual conclusions are very different from the beginning observations.

"You know, looking back now, it is hard for me to believe that Lincoln replaced McClellan after Sharpsburg," Colonel Paul observed.

"Wow, Colonel, that is a bold statement," Doc Greene chimed in. As usual Doc Greene was listening to everyone's conversations while pretending to be completely aloof from all.

George agreed. "McClellan really did not have that great of a track record," he added.

Colonel Paul chuckled. "History has been very unkind to George McClellan. No, he was not Stonewall, Longstreet, Grant, or Sherman but he was a much better General than he is given credit for."

Doc Greene knew better than to question the authority of this war veteran, but he just could not help a little ribbing, "Colonel, maybe we need to check you over again. I think your memory may be fading just a touch." Colonel Paul grinned. "Ahhh, young doctor, my memory is just fine, but my sanity, now that is the question."

Everyone got a good laugh. George knew exactly to what the Colonel was referring. Everyone thought Colonel Paul was touched with just a little insanity from the war. The fact that he spent most mornings and some afternoons in a cemetery often mumbling to himself had furthered that belief. Normally, that would be a reputation well earned, but George knew better. Had the good townspeople been through what the Colonel had, they most likely would have never survived it.

"Who are those Texans, Colonel?" George said, "those boys you go visit in the mornings."

"I don't rightly know, George. I'm not sure if they were soldiers with me in the Eastern Theatre or not. They could have been with us at some point with Hood in the Devil's Den, or maybe they were with us at Chickamauga as river of death gunmen. They could have been with Cleburne, known as the Stonewall of the West, or they might have been westerners defending Atlanta with Granbury, some of Waco's best."

George decided that one day he would discover who those Texas soldiers were that had died and been buried in Auburn.

"Whoever those soldiers were, no doubt they would agree with me, a very sane and rational doctor, that McClellan was not a fine general of the highest quality," Doc Greene interrupted.

"Listen, Doc, McClellan pushed us out of Maryland. Up until that time no one had been able to slow General Lee and our role in ending the war. And just take a good look at what came after his replacement . . . Burnside and his blunders."

There was little arguing with that point. Anyone who had ever heard the stories knew Fredericksburg was one federal blunder after another. Colonel Paul had given several lectures to students about the subject. Doc knew better than to go any further. Over time, Colonel Paul's lectures on the defensive genius of Longstreet's brand of war had become well known. The absolute zenith of this study was shown at Fredericksburg. Case in point, the Colonel would argue with anyone that this battle proved that given enough time and the ground of their choosing, Longstreet, under the watchful eye of Lee, could never have been driven from the field.

"Colonel, did you see him?" George asked.

"Who, George?"

"Robert Marye."

With a deep sigh, Colonel Paul responded, "I did."

"Remarkable."

"He really was a ray of light, an angel. Our staff was mixed in with Hood and Longstreet on top of a hill after the battle in observation. The Yankees had come in wave after wave under Burnside's orders.

They crashed into the wall carved into the heights that now bear his name only to be beaten back time and time again. You know they were Irish federals fighting Irish rebels down there? There had to be family members, cousins at least, killing each other." At that the colonel stopped for a few seconds. Tears slowly began to build in his eyes. After a few moments of silence, he continued, "The federals were finished on that side of the battlefield. We all had our binoculars scanning the field when a captain in Longstreet's staff spotted him. 'Look!' the man screamed while pointing in the direction of the carnage. A South Carolinian soldier had crawled over the wall after the battle to give water to the wounded enemy slowly dying in agony in front of him.

Not knowing we were witnessing one of the greatest examples of humanity in history, we sat in silence and stared. I'm not sure how the other men felt, but I thanked God that day for that man, the Angel of Marye's Heights. May we all one day show such loving mercy and a human touch to one another."

—16—

As the train pulled into Newnan station, Dr. George Petrie had several things on his mind. Motivation had been a subject for a few days now leading up to the game. He had been scribbling some words here and there in anticipation of giving the boys a speech before the game. He thought this might better explain to people why he thought the game today was so important. On the ride thus far, George had taken many thoughts to heart. Not just things that had been shared by the Colonel, but by anyone he had interacted with that morning. What made him such a great scholar was that he was always observing.

When the train came to a halt, the sun had finally overcome the clouds and the day began to reveal itself to be almost perfect for this time of year. Although the wind still blustered in spurts, everyone was certain that a calm in the weather was coming later in the afternoon. At the station, the passengers fled the stuffy train cars and meandered outside for a break. Tables were set up and the people from Auburn broke out picnic baskets with a wealth of food to enjoy. The students were most appreciative of the meal. Even Colonel Paul, closely followed by both Buck and Doc Greene, stepped outside for a breath of fresh air. The mayor spotted the Colonel and had his wife rush over to invite him to their portable meal.

"Colonel, will you please come join us for a quick bite before we continue?" she asked politely, and not to be rude, he accepted. However, Doc Greene did not. He gave the mayor's wife a smile and a wink and without a word moved toward a card game that had begun further down the platform.

Buck accompanied the Colonel to the table. Although he could not sit down to eat, there was no way Colonel Paul was going to get out of his sight in case anything happened again.

"Mr. Mayor, how are you?" asked the Colonel while extending his hand.

"Fine, sir," the mayor replied. "I did not know we had a soldier accompanying us today. What do you think of this whole deal?" the mayor inquired.

But before the Colonel could answer, the mayor continued talking as the Colonel listened to what was obviously a prepared speech which basically dismissed the whole event as some sort of quackery. William Paul knew enough about politicians to know that they only ask questions they think they already know the answers to, and the best thing to do is to nod, smile, and cross your arms when they get on a roll like this one.

After a quick bite to eat, the Colonel, still shadowed by Buck, politely dismissed himself from the table. He was ready to move back to the safety and obscurity of the back of the train but George caught his eye. George who had been checking on his boys was now alone at the other end of the platform and appeared to be writing something. *He looks stuck*, Colonel Paul thought. He was going to let his friend be but then decided he had better check on him.

Colonel Paul made his way over and interrupted him with, "How goes it Young Captain?"

George had a look of worry on his face. "I'm sort of scared, Colonel."

It takes a lot for any man, especially one of George's stature, to admit they are scared. Colonel Paul knew this about his friend, which is probably why George admitted it to him. The Young Captain had a right to be nervous. He was responsible for this trip. If it did not go well, the mayor and the other doubters would have all the ammunition they needed to dismiss this venture permanently. The weight of this whole exhibition was squarely on the young scholar's shoulders.

"Can't blame you. Not at all, George," the Colonel said. "If the whole thing goes bad, the mayor and all of them will blame you."

George responded in earnest, "I'm not scared of that or them. They can have the town. I am worried about letting down my boys. For weeks now they have sacrificed their time, their efforts, their sweat and blood for a game. What if I let them down today? Colonel, I really do not even know what to say to them before the game. Do I say anything at all? Do I yell, scream, or push them into a frenzy? Do I just leave them alone and trust they will execute what we have worked and planned for? I've been searching for some words, but cannot seem to find a way to describe to them what I feel about today."

Colonel Paul thought for a minute before answering. Knowing this was immensely important to his friend, he wanted to choose his words carefully. The fact of the matter was that he knew exactly what George was feeling. He had felt that same doubt countless times during his life as a soldier. Doubt was dangerous. Doubt was deadly to life. Doubt was the devil.

"George, you are a good person with an even better heart," he began. "I am proud to know you and I am proud of you. There are very few people in this world with a positive vision, and you can count yourself as one of them. When we get to Union, I want you to leave us in the back and join your team for the rest of the ride to Atlanta. You sit them down and tell them to start concentrating on their future jobs for the day. Have them visualize what they need to execute while you slowly walk up and down the aisle, look each of them in the eye, and tell them what they need to hear."

George took a deep breath and asked, "What is that?"

Colonel Paul sat down next to his friend, patted him on the back and said, "Tell them why you love this world. Tell them about honesty, loyalty, and truthfulness. Tell them how proud you are of them for taking the extra time to be here and for the hard work they have put in for this cause. Tell them that we will never be split again like we once were, because this country is special. They are special because of this country. Tell them that they are part of something as a team that is bigger than the individual, and let them know that they are a family. No matter what, no matter where they came from before now, they are now Auburn men for life and you love them for it."

The train whistle broke up the conversation and all the festivities at the station. The conductor yelled, "All aboard," and everyone began to make their way back to the train. George did not move. Colonel Paul told Buck to go on ahead and he would get back to his seat in time. Grudgingly, Buck obliged. The platform all but cleared except for William and George. George stood up, looked at his friend with tears in his eyes, and said, "Thank you, Colonel. I know what to do now."

Colonel Paul nodded. He knew his friend could do anything. The two made their way to the train just in time.

"Let's ride," Colonel Paul said with a smile and the two men hopped back on the train destined for Atlanta.

—17—

As the conductor pulled the train's whistle to let everyone know that it was time to embark further on the journey, George hastily made his way to the back train car. Colonel Paul and Doc Greene were in the very back of the car shadowed closely by Buck's watchful eyes. George could not help but notice that several more groups of people had joined the trip and it was exciting. There was a growing buzz in the air and he started to realize that it was in anticipation of today's game.

He also could not help but notice that his friend Colonel Paul appeared to be feeling better. Perhaps the breath of fresh air during the recent stop had been good for him. He and his old friend Doc Greene looked as chipper as two young school boys ready to cause some small trouble in the back of an elementary school classroom. George scribbled a few more words down on paper and then decided to rejoin his travel mates in the back of the car.

"Petrie, do you need Buck and me to keep an eye on you the rest of the way as well?" Doc Greene exclaimed.

It was blatantly obvious that the Doc's chipper behavior was being elevated by his imbibing in more of the Colonel's flask.

"Now Doc," Colonel Paul interrupted, "the Young Captain is very ready for the task at hand."

"Truth be known, gentlemen," George responded, "I have not been this nervous since my finals at John Hopkins."

Hoping to take his young friend's mind off his worries, the Colonel decided to tell a story he had never shared with anyone, not even his deceased wife. He was not sure if it would help calm his young friend's nerves, but maybe he could learn something from it. Or maybe he just needed to personally get this off his chest.

"George, you know I have seen the absolute worst in people during my time in the Civil War." There is a fear in some of those moments that torment me to this day. One time, in Gettysburg,

General Lee had unfortunately decided that our part of the army needed to take a hill called Little Round Top."

Doc, Buck, George and everyone within hearing distance in the car turned their attention directly to Colonel Paul.

"It was bloody bad ground. The locals had named the rock formation close to the base of the small mountain "The Devil's Den." They called it that because for as long as people had lived in the area, going as far back as the native Indians, there was folklore that a giant serpent lived in those rocks." Colonel Paul stopped for a moment, took a deep breath and a small pull from his flask before continuing. "Now I do not know if there were any demons really living in that patch of hell, but bullets, shells, and shattered rock made a sound like a serpent hissing on that day."

Gettysburg, George thought. Other than the signing of the Declaration of Independence, is there a more important day in American History? George knew that the Colonel was a very special man, but a Gettysburg survivor? He could not help but momentarily contemplate the significance of that. Without knowing it, the Colonel's story had the effect he was hoping for. George was not thinking, and therefore not worrying, about what was to come later in the day.

"Now, General Hood had argued with Longstreet and Lee almost all morning about this charge to take the hill. He begged, pleaded, and worked his words into a fury about how costly this maneuver would be."

George knew this to be true from his study of history. Although very few of his peers would ever admit it, Lee made a big mistake at Gettysburg. The federals had a huge advantage in the terrain they held that old warriors like the Colonel called "the high ground." The Confederates should have followed Longstreet's advice to Lee, disengaged, flanked the Yanks, positioned themselves in between the Union army and their capital, and then chosen the ground on which they wanted to fight a possible last battle of the war.

"Longstreet knew this to be a bad fight. He did not want any part of the fight there at the Devil's Den, but he was overruled."

"What if you would have carried that hill top, Colonel?"

"We would have won the war."

The Colonel painted an almost romantic picture of the Confederate Army led by Hood carrying Little Round Top and then the entire Army of the Potomac falling like dominoes lined up on their ends in a neat row. Thousands of Texans, Alabamians, then Virginians and North Carolinians swarming like ants over the Maine boys, and the New Yorkers, and then the boys from Wisconsin and Pennsylvania. Instead, the plan failed miserably and that was the beginning of the end for the Southern Army.

"Like I said earlier, Hood was irate. I was with him as he and Longstreet yelled at each other about duty, honor, and several other words I will not repeat. At the end, Hood frustratedly turned to me, ordered me to help him carry the field and we, along with several other officers, rallied the men who were stalled in the Devil's Den."

Colonel Paul suddenly felt the need to stand up. He put his left hand on Buck's muscular shoulder and leaned his weight onto his friend. "Buck, I guess that is why I visit the cemetery almost every morning."

"What you mean, Colonel?"

"Because I should have been put in a grave that day." The Colonel felt a chill come over him as he explained what it was like inside the den of death. Very quickly, both he and Hood had been jolted from their horses by shrapnel. Hood would almost lose an arm and be lost for much of the rest of the war. The Colonel, still a Major at this time, recovered from his jolt and led men out of the Den while pushing toward Round Top. He was hit again in the arm and left wounded at the base of the hill.

"Was you scared, Colonel?"

"You know, Buck, I was. Somehow, I crawled up on a rock at the rim of the Devil's Den to wait for the serpent to come take me. Despite the summer heat, the rock I lay upon was quite cool. I could not hear well because of the blast that had knocked me off my horse earlier. But I could see, and it was horrible."

"What did you see?" inquired Doc Greene.

"Well, I did not see any serpents or demons if that is what you are asking. But I tell you, it was the blood. It was everywhere. It pooled up like water left behind from a tidal wave. It was deep in the craters of those rocks."

"Hard to tell whose blood it was, eh, Colonel?" Doc Greene interjected.

"Well, men, southern or northern, no matter from what state, Texas or Alabama, it was all red there on that hot July day," Colonel Paul said soberly. "They say that to this day, even after all the years of rain and decay that blood, especially from the men of Alabama and Texas, still stains those rocks like some crimson tide from that terrible day."

—18—

By George's rough count, Colonel Paul had fought in at least four of the most significant battles in the Eastern Theatre of the American Civil War. There was Second Manassas, Antietam, Fredericksburg, and Gettysburg. George asked about Chancellorsville, but the Colonel, along with many other Texans, had missed out on the glory of that one.

"We were on loan down in Suffolk for what would later be known as Longstreet's tidewater operations. More than anything that meant we were to go out to forage for supplies to feed Lee's entire army. Who knew we would miss Lee wrecking Hooker up in northern Virginia!"

The train was now a few miles outside of Union and therefore maybe only about one hour south of Atlanta and Petrie's moment with destiny. The game was scheduled to begin at 3:30 that afternoon. George took the watch from his front shirt pocket and read 1:30. He knew they were now only two hours away from the beginning of Auburn football. The thought of the opening kick made Dr. Petrie's stomach feel a little queasy. At this he nervously asked Colonel Paul, "Were there any other battles in the east you fought or missed out on?"

"Well, Young Captain, I did miss out on the aftermath of Gettysburg in the east and fortunately did not partake in any of the Wilderness, Petersburg, or Appomattox. If you remember your history, you will recall that many of us, Texans mainly, were caught up in north Georgia after our defeat in Pennsylvania."

Yes, how foolish of me, George thought. *What a silly question.* He began to blush when the Colonel spoke up. "It's all right, George, I lived through it all and still mix up the timeline of events."

George smiled appreciatively. "What transpired after Gettysburg?"

"I was left for dead at the base of Little Round Top. Scouts under a flag of truce to bury the dead found me that night. They were southern scouts and when they realized I was still barely alive, they took me to the field hospital. My old friend Alan was there looking for me, too, and basically fought the tent surgeon off from taking my mangled arm. They cleaned the wound as best they could and the pain was so intense that I passed out. The next thing I remember was waking up in a cart being pulled by two horses with other wounded men while being evacuated south after the battle had officially ended."

"Sounds miserable," Doc Greene added.

"It was. Every time we hit a bump in that cart the pain shot through my arm. When we finally stopped, I made myself walk the rest of the way. My legs were fine, it was just my arm that hurt so terribly. I think if I had stayed in that cart I would have just balled up and died."

Colonel Paul went on to explain that the rest of the time after Gettysburg was a blur. Although it took only a week to get back to Virginia, it felt like many weeks had elapsed. "Time seemed to stop as we all recovered from that beating."

Having never failed in his life, George had a hard time understanding the feeling of complete loss. It was difficult to listen to the Colonel describe the feeling of devastation. He began again to worry about the upcoming game, and if there would be a similar blur afterwards as the Colonel had described. To refocus himself to something more positive, George spoke up.

"Colonel, did you move with Longstreet to Chickamauga?"

Colonel Paul smiled. "Ah, Young Captain, you have regained your memory of history. That is exactly what happened."

—19—

As the train pulled into Union station, five miles south of Atlanta, Colonel Paul instructed Buck to find him some more rum or brandy to fill his flask. He had not thought about Chickamauga in years—maybe not even since it happened. People often forget that there were several theatres involved in the American Civil War—the Eastern Theatre with Lee, the seas and rivers. Men fought in Arkansas, Missouri, Ohio, and Kentucky. Anywhere that northern men and southern men were approximated to one another, they tried to kill each other. And nowhere was that more true than in north Georgia in the Western Theatre of the war.

Colonel Paul explained that as much glory as is shown to the east in the American Civil War that the west was of equal importance if not more. "People seem to forget just how important those deep south states were to the cause of southern independence."

"How is that?" George asked.

"Well, much of the deep south was not touched by the northern forces. Therefore, the farms there were intact and producing at levels much higher than pre-war, the cotton especially. It was not just cotton though. Those farms also produced everything from corn to hemp which were all desperately needed for the effort."

George knew this to be true. He also knew that northern men like Sherman and Grant knew this as well. They wanted to extend the war to Mississippi, Alabama, Georgia, and South Carolina as quickly as possible. If they could not take the head off the snake in Virginia, George knew from his studies they wanted to disembowel the body.

"And let me guess, Colonel, Atlanta was the key to that northern control?"

"Absolutely. Just like we will fight those Georgia boys today for the city, men fought over it thirty years ago."

"Hell," Doc Greene interrupted, "we will probably be fighting those Georgia boys and others for it a hundred years from now!"

Everyone got a good laugh from the doctor's proclamation. Colonel Paul thought for a second and replied, "You are probably right, Doctor. You are probably right."

Through all this conversation the men had failed to notice all the passengers squeezing onto the train. Every car was packed now. Colonel Paul started telling a story about the incredible logistical feat that took place for Longstreet to move practically his entire army from outside Richmond, Virginia, to Dalton, Georgia, to aid in the fight against the Union Army led by General Rosecrans. "We moved mountains to get down to Georgia. Ole Braxton Bragg was in real trouble and after Gettysburg, Lee thought it a good idea to dispatch Longstreet from the Army of Northern Virginia."

"Why was that, Colonel?"

"A lot of the other Generals blamed the loss at Gettysburg on Longstreet. Especially the more vocal ones like dumb Jubal Early. Lee figured the best way to resolve the issue was to shelve Longstreet for a while, and let things cool over in his absence."

"So, the train rides to Georgia, is that why you told me earlier in the week you don't care for train travel?" George asked.

"That definitely has something to do with it."

"Chickamauga, what happened there, Colonel?"

"Well, it ended the war for me as I knew it."

By the time the Colonel had ended up in north Georgia, he had been promoted from Major to Lt. Colonel. Unlike most of his fellow officers, he had survived Gettysburg and the promotion was due to attrition as much as anything. But, in the Texas infantries in the east, the men who did the fighting had a lot of say about who their leaders would be. The truth is the men cared for William Paul. He was a fighter. They honored him by electing him a Colonel.

"My arm was still injured so they allowed me some help. Naturally, I asked my friend Alan to be my aide. We still had contact with the men, but like at Fredericksburg before, I was assigned to aid General Hood as much as possible in more staff work."

"General Hood was back with the Army?"

"Yes, he was in worse shape than me, but the men were thrilled to have him back again. He was thrilled to be back with them, also."

"And you were all with Longstreet still, even after the dustup at Gettysburg?"

"We were. Despite the differences from time to time, we always had much respect for General Longstreet. Although he had a hard time sometimes showing it, that man loved his men more than anything, even more than his own family, I think."

"What about General Bragg?"

"We hated him. He was a real piece of work."

The men indeed hated General Bragg. Colonel Paul thought that even General Bragg hated General Bragg. He went on to explain that he was not a horrible General, but just an all-around horrible leader. He was quick to judge and quick to look for blame. He refused to entertain any other ideas or intelligence and he basically displayed no loyalty to any other officer on his staff.

"He was a back biter."

"Bloody Bragg," Doc Greene mumbled, "almost as intolerable as Sherman himself."

"The sad thing is Doc, he was a talented military mind, but he was just paranoid." Colonel Paul said.

"Maybe that is why Lee sent Longstreet," George interjected, "to calm Bragg."

Colonel Paul laughed. "Maybe George, just maybe."

He was back in Chickamauga on the eve of battle. Colonel Paul was with Alan. All the southern leaders had gathered together behind the line of battle opposite of the Union Army and Rosecrans. Hood was there along with Longstreet and several other staff officers. Bragg had come up on horseback to discuss the situation. Longstreet mainly listened with a poker face. "We kept our distance from General Longstreet until Bragg left him to inspect further down the line. It appeared then that Longstreet was thankful for our presence and rode over to our group.

With a smile, Longstreet said 'General Hood, is this the soldier who stole the Carolinians' wagons back at Manassas?'

'General, may I introduce Colonel William Paul?'

'Colonel Paul, it is nice to meet you. Do you think if we wreck poor "Rosey" over there today you can let us have some of their wagons?'

General Longstreet, it is an honor to meet you, I said. How about we enjoy our last cigars first, and then see about destroying General Rosecrans afterwards."

Longstreet nodded approvingly.

"I instructed Alan to fetch my last cigars for the two generals. Alan produced three and for a few minutes we enjoyed the bonding as if we were in some bar without a care in the world. With the cigar offering, both Longstreet and Hood momentarily let down their guards and swapped even older war stories from West Point, Mexico, and on the range against Indians."

"Imagine it, George, a young man from Nacogdoches, Texas, sitting horseback on a small mound smoking a cigar with two of the greatest American generals in history." A slightly jealous George asked, "How did it end?"

—20—

As the train sat in Union station, George listened intently to what would be the last of Colonel Paul's Civil War stories for the day. In all honesty, his thoughts had been turning for his own task in Atlanta for the better part of the last half of this trip. Thoughts of both triumph and the agony of possible defeat began to run through his mind. Focus now was the key. Win the game or lose it, the process to victory began with a focus on each part of the game being played correctly. Nevertheless, he was not quite ready to unleash his famous focus in full just yet. There was one more thing he wanted to hear about while he had the chance. He might never have this opportunity again, and it was important to understand Chickamauga from real experience.

"Well, like I said, I was in the saddle enjoying the last of my cigars, listening to Hood and Longstreet trade stories. We were all positioned on a small knoll looking over the north Georgia terrain and not really focused in on the battlefield sprawled below us. I was enthralled by the stories between the two men. Hood was telling Longstreet, a talented poker player himself, about winning a large sum of money pre-war on a Kentucky river boat paddling down the Mississippi."

George looked over at Doc Greene, who was now completely dialed into the conversation because of the mention of large sums of money being wagered.

The Colonel knew he had a captive audience waiting for his briefing of the action. Taking the opportunity for a dramatic pause, he reached for his flask, took a small sip of the sweet rum inside of it and then passed it around to the men situated nearby. Each man in turn took a small sip, except for Dr. Petrie, before passing the flask along like they were being initiated into a secret club. Once the flask made its way back to the Colonel, he took a final sip, recorked the flask and put it back into his coat pocket.

"Now I have never told this story to anyone before . . . so here goes.

It was a cool September morning up there in those north Georgia mountains. We were all laughing at Hood's story as he described the wife of one of the men in the poker match storming into the room where they were playing and slapping her husband across the back of the head for losing all their money. Hood described her as a 'big, whale-like woman' and the poor little fella 'was this skinny, red-headed donk' who could not be shamed into leaving the table.

While I was laughing along at the story, I glanced over to Alan who was not paying any attention to General Hood at all."

"What was he doing, Colonel?"

"He was observing the enemy lines through his binoculars. I shifted my horse around the generals, and the joyful crowd that had gathered around the two men, and made my way about thirty feet over to Alan who was quietly alone in observation."

"What was he looking at?" George quizzed.

"You see, George, sometimes you have to look for the signs. Call it providence, your guardian angel nudging you in a direction to move, a sixth sense, a gut instinct, or what the Indians call visions. Some folks call them haints. There are signs given from time to time in your life that show you the way. Some people are more in touch with those signs than others."

George interrupted, "And Alan was one of those people?"

"Yes, he was. He must have had some Indian blood in him to go along with that Irish blood. He was eerily silent looking through those glasses. It was almost like he was the only person on the field.

As I made my way over to him, a chill ran over my body—a sensation, the old timers called it."

"Alan," I said, "just what are you studying over so hard?"

"An eagle, sir."

"An eagle?"

"Yes sir, a war eagle."

"A *war* eagle?"

"Yes, sir. My father told me of the elder Irishmen from the old country speaking stories about eagles and hawks appearing on the battlefield when the Romans invaded. They were Irish spirits who showed the men where to attack."

"Irish spirits, Alan? More like bedtime stories. Give me Wheeler and Forrest in Cavalry and I will show you exactly where to attack."

"Look for yourself, sir," he said confidently while handing his lookers to me.

A few of the other soldiers surrounding the generals had moved over near Alan and me. I raised those binoculars to eye level and peered across the battlefield where Alan had said the eagle had been circling above the federal lines. Sure enough, a mature golden eagle could be seen above the line. The bird had a gigantic wing span of at least six feet and was covered from beak to talon in stunning, reddish brown feathers."

George interrupted, "Colonel, what else did you see?"

Buck had noticed the Colonel had gone into some type of trance while telling this story. He moved closer to him in anticipation of him having another spell.

"George, it was so peaceful. This beautiful bird of prey hovering above the blue coats and rising on the warm air currents below. I looked at the bird for what seemed like an eternity, and then saw it."

"What did you see Colonel? Was it a haint?" Buck asked.

—21—

The Colonel, now fully immersed in remembrance, continued with the story.

"Oh my God."

"Now do you see it, sir?"

Colonel Paul had seen it, but he could not believe it. Alan was right. The war eagle had just revealed their path to victory. Below where the majestic eagle had been hovering, a hole began to open in the federal line. What had first appeared to be a small space no larger than two or three men had widened quickly to the size of a squad, then a company, and finally to a brigade-sized hole in the federal line of battle. Just below where the eagle circled, General Thomas Wood had been mistakenly ordered to move his troops off the line by Commanding General Rosecrans.

Colonel Paul did not wait for orders. He dropped the glasses and took off in a full gallop on his horse toward the gap. Other soldiers nearby on horseback had noticed the Colonel and Alan, and followed the lone rider excitedly. Both Longstreet and Hood startled from their reverie raised their spectacles toward the fleeing soldiers and saw the hole as well. Longstreet had been preparing his men all morning for an attack. Quickly, he gave the official orders to do so.

"Follow that Texan, follow that Texan!" Longstreet could be heard over the entire battlefield while waving his hat in excitement. "Follow that damn war eagle!"

Not to be outdone in any circumstances, Hood also turned toward the gap. He rushed into it with all of his might rallying confederate troops toward the breach.

From his studies, George knew well of this maneuver. The confederates stacked up in a narrow column much like a spear and exploited the breach in the federal lines with an aggressive thrust. What he never knew was that at the tip of that "spear" was an old soldier currently sitting at the back of this train—someone that many of the good townspeople of Auburn thought might be moderately insane.

"So, Colonel, you were at the vanguard of Longstreet's attack at Chickamauga?"

"No, Young Captain, I *was* the vanguard of Longstreet's attack at Chickamauga."

The Colonel took a deep breath and looked around the train car. There was complete silence. Everyone crowded around him was staring in complete shock. The Colonel scratched his beard for a few seconds, thought it might be a good time to have another drink, and pulled the flask out from his coat pocket. After he took a sip, he offered the flask up to everyone again but for some reason they all declined this go around.

"Well, more for me I guess. And there it is. An old Irish myth as ancient as the Romans signaled the way of one of the greatest tactical moves in Civil War history. Kind of hard to believe, right Young Captain?"

"Not if you know how to read the signs," George said.

And with a nod and a look of admiration, the Colonel said, "Very good."

The train prepared to move out of Union Station and the next stop would be Atlanta, and the day's destiny.

"I think it is time, Colonel," George said. The Young Captain then stood up, shook the Colonel's hand and started moving through the crowded train car toward the car where his team was waiting.

"Yes, it is, George. Yes, my friend, it is your time," said the Colonel proudly.

—22—

As the train roared north to Atlanta, George made his way into the team car. It was full of students, and crowds of new riders in addition to the players. Lots of unfamiliar faces gazed at him as he made his way to the front of the car where the team was positioned. Several players asked, out of respect, if he wanted their seats, but George declined. The players noticed an unusual look on Dr. Petrie's face. This was a look they had never seen before. Their coach appeared to be ready to go into war.

There had also been a nervousness for the team during the train ride. With every stop at every station, and the closer the train moved toward Atlanta, the more nervous the men felt. It was a relief to some extent to see on the face of their coach that he meant business. This was an entirely new venture to them also, and not one person on this train, except Dr. Petrie, knew what to expect. Outside of witnessing a few games, the Young Captain was inexperienced, but the boys did not need to know that.

Now only a few miles south of Atlanta, Dr. Petrie asked some of the players to help him move many of the passengers out of their car and into some of the others. They needed a few minutes by themselves, quietly together, to focus before they arrived in Atlanta. A few of the riders objected, but most of them moved to other cars. One or two of the disgruntled riders moved into the car where Colonel Paul was riding with Doc and Buck. Upon seeing them, the Colonel gave up his seat, directed Doc to do the same and motioned for all three of them to move into the car with the team. The three men silently made their way to the back of the team car and directed their attention and support toward George. The Colonel liked what he saw.

George had his team in seats in the front of the car on both sides of the aisle. The Young Captain was walking up and down the aisle in a confident manner calmly talking to his team about their game plan. The train was now in Atlanta moving closer to Piedmont Park.

"You must tackle in mass, men," the Colonel heard George say. "Swarm to the ball. Put the ball carrier on the ground forcefully. Offensive line, you have to push those Georgia players off the line, again and again," he was saying. "And on the defensive side, no one pushes us back. Hold the line. Never to yield. Do not surrender. Do not quit, ever," George insisted.

The Colonel thought he could have been on a hillside being shelled at Gettysburg, and George could not have been leading his men any better.

They were getting close to the last stop. George could see the city. The train was beginning to slow down. This was his last chance to get some words of encouragement to his team. The Young Captain began to speak with tears welling in his eyes.

"Men, Auburn men. I want to thank you for your hard work and practice over the last few months. You know I believe in hard work, and no one could make me prouder of your effort than you men have made me. Today we represent a university, the education and knowledge that it grants us. You all know how I feel about education and how much I believe in it. You have done more than train your minds, you have also worked on training your bodies. You have grown together spiritually and have used your training to develop the skills that God has gifted each of you with. You are the total man now. I have watched you work. I have observed a lot of people on this trip today display a real human touch like yours, and it brings me true happiness. We have all been through a lot in our lives. We have come from different places, some as far as Texas, Virginia, and all over to be here humbly today. That is what the Auburn spirit is all about. No matter where any of us are from, this university will always be our home. No matter what happens on the field today, win or lose, you all are Auburn men and winners to me. I can see in your eyes that you feel the same way about it that I do, and I want you to know because you believe in this also, I love you for it!"

And with that, the train pulled up to the last stop for the day. A silence fell over the car as George made his way to the door to lead his team off the train. No one noticed the massive crowds that were outside waiting at the station. It felt like no one in the car could move. Finally, Colonel Paul stood up to disembark. George looked at him and asked, "Would you like to add something, Colonel?"

The entire team swiveled their heads toward the back of the car and looked at Colonel Paul.

The Colonel smiled and yelled out, "LAST MAN STANDING YELLS WAR EAGLE, LET'S GO!"

The team erupted.

—23—

Just like a true leader, George stepped off the train first followed by Colonel Paul. A massive crowd was continuing to gather around the train depot. It was like the entire city had made its way toward Piedmont Park to watch this inaugural game. The time was now three o'clock and the team was thirty minutes away from Auburn Football.

The crowd had zero effect on George Petrie. He had a laser focus and sternly, but deftly, moved through it as people began to open a hole for him to pass like Rosecrans did for the southerners at Chickamauga.

Colonel Paul, on the other hand, was in complete awe. This was not the Atlanta he had been evacuated from on his death bed by rail car in 1864. That is how he had come to Auburn. After charging first into the gap created by Rosecrans at Chickamauga the Colonel, followed by thousands of other screaming furies from all around the south, pushed what felt like almost all the way to Chattanooga. He had not had time to finish the story of Chickamauga, and subsequently what happened to him there. The Colonel stopped for just a minute to reflect. He said to himself and to God, *This is the last time I think about this.*

Amongst the noise of the crowd, William Paul bowed his head slightly, and relived the moment. He had pushed miles into the breach along with many other men. They kept moving rapidly, fighting and killing anything blue in sight. This felt like the opportunity to finally end the war and for all that the Rebels had missed so many times before. It was savagery. It was brutal. The Colonel had a few tears begin to well in his eyes while remembering the destruction.

"Oh God, I'm so sorry," he said quietly.

And then the thrust had ended as quickly as it had begun. A tough, southern-born commander who stayed loyal to the north had formed one last line at Horseshoe Ridge and stopped the onslaught. Colonel Paul had reached as far as he would go in the war, and what seemed at the time, possibly in life. He was hit by a shell while attacking George Henry Thomas's position at the base of the ridge and that was it.

Colonel Paul, near death, was evacuated by Alan to the rear and later taken to a hospital in Atlanta to recover. Months later he was evacuated to the Texas field hospital at a small university in Auburn, Alabama, as General Sherman moved to take the city. He never saw his young friend Alan again.

"C-c-colonel?" Buck stammered.

"William!" Doc Greene shouted.

Buck and Doc Greene had followed the team off the train and finally caught up to the Colonel. There would be no catching up with George. He was marching toward the park on a mission. The Colonel came out of his quiet reverie and smiled at the two men. They could tell he had been crying.

"You good, sir?" Buck asked with compassion.

"It's done," the Colonel replied.

"What is?"

But the Colonel said nothing more. Doc Greene knew what the Colonel meant. After a brief pause to clear his mind of worry, Buck did as well. All three of these men had seen death in their own ways up close and personal—the Colonel in war, the Doctor in treatments, and Buck in his neglected community. They all knew the look of someone finally taking the good Lord's mercy once and for all.

"It has been a great ride and I am very humbled and fortunate to have enjoyed it with you two," the Colonel said.

Doc Greene replied, "It sure has, William." Buck nodded in agreement and smiled. He was grateful to have earned the respect of his fellow men.

At that moment a drunken mob of students from Georgia Tech University started pushing through the crowd. The three men looked on at the sight of the students with both amazement and peculiarity. It was not just students from Tech, but from all around the south. People came from Oxford, Mississippi and the university there. Birmingham, Alabama had a trainload. People from Tennessee, North Carolina, and from all parts of Georgia were there. The trio realized suddenly that they were part of something bigger than themselves. Bigger than the city they had come from. This was a happening.

They also realized that their momentary pause had caused them to lose sight of George, the football team, and most of the East Alabama train population that they had travelled with.

Doc spoke first. "Well, Mr. Civil War hero, which way to the game?"

"I guess we just follow the crowd," the Colonel responded.

"Splendid advice," Doc cackled.

"Well my friends, when you are lost in a crowd, see where it takes you." At this point, he could have cared less where it took him. This entire trip had been one wild emotional ride that had been building inside of him for almost forty years. He felt cleansed. This was not the Atlanta in shambles he saw during the end of his war. This was a living, breathing organism with a strong beating heart. It was not just rebuilt. It was booming! People were everywhere. Happy people not stained by the depression of war, they had wonderful looks on their faces. It was fresh. *Damn*, he thought, *they look hopeful.*

Buck had taken the time to climb on a small trash can to see over the crowd. In the distance, he could see clearly the direction the crowd was lumbering toward and if his eyes did not mistake him, the silhouette of what looked to be grandstands.

"That way," Buck pointed.

The Colonel approved. "Good scouting, Buck. I could have used you at Gettysburg," he said.

Climbing down, Buck replied, "No thanks, Colonel. I like living and sure would not have wanted to see no Devil's Den!"

Doc Greene spotted a newspaper in the can that Buck had descended from. The trashcan was overflowing now from all the travelers' trash and the newspaper sat on top of it.

"Look here now," he said with a smile. It was an article in the local Atlanta newspaper entitled: FIRST COLLEGE GAME EVER: GA STATE vs API.

The three men started making their way toward the park. Doc kept reading the article while navigating the crowd.

"3,000–5,000 people expected. They are playing for a silver cup and people are expected from all over the south," Doc murmured. "Bloody hell," he said. "I need another drink!"

—24—

George was exactly where he was supposed to be. Walking through the grandstands and entering the football field where the game would be played today. It was a lovely sight. For a moment he let his focus on his task wane to embrace the pageantry. It was now 3:15 and the team was fifteen minutes away from Auburn Football.

Not only were the grandstands filling, hundreds of people were surrounding the field on small inclines and ridges around the park. They were drinking, eating, cheering, yelling, and some even fighting like it was some giant party. George bowed his head for a second and thought *God, I sure do love it. This life. Thank you for this happening.* Relieved with the turnout and now fully knowing that not only all debts would be paid off from the massive crowd's ticket sales, but that they would turn some profit, he turned his attention to his team filing into the park.

George made his way over to them. They circled him and he directed his young captain Wright to take them to their sideline. He also directed the team to begin warming up for the game. They immediately turned to do his bidding. They were ready and he knew it.

For a brief moment, George looked for the Colonel. He could not see his friend who, unbeknownst to George, was still caught up in the crowd making its way to the park. He was worried for a brief second but took a deep breath and began his legendary focus again for the task at hand.

Then he heard it. The Georgia boys had arrived in all their glory. The team came dressed in a bright red and deep coal black uniform. They had a band led by drummers pounding so hard that it sounded like thunder. Their team had a mascot. "A damn billy goat!" someone in the crowd yelled. The one thing that George noticed in the entire spectacle, more than anything, was their fans. He thought to himself that they barked like a pack of dogs. Loud, unruly, and brutishly, they screamed at their opponents with every obscenity known to man. It made chills run down his spine.

As the Georgia tallyho slithered their way into Piedmont Park, George noticed his old friend Dr. Herty begin to make his way onto the football field. He was walking briskly toward the middle of the field so Dr. Petrie moved in that direction as well. A few referees for the game started to make their way to meet the coaches. It was now 3:25 p.m. and the team was five minutes away from Auburn football.

"George, by God we did it," Dr. Herty said while extending his hand. They shook hands and George replied, "Good to see you, my friend." The two embraced and looked more like long lost brothers than football coaches.

The refs gathered around and the rules of the game were hashed out. They explained to the two coaches that there would be two halves to the game. The clock would run for each half for seventy minutes continuously. Neither team would be allotted any time outs. There would be three chances called "downs" to make five yards. If five yards could not be made, the team would relinquish control of the football to the other team. If any player in the game was hurt, after the play, that player would be escorted off the field and a replacement could be made. To score points, each team must move the ball past the other team's "goal line" to be awarded a total of four points. After that score, an extra two-point play from three yards out would be allowed. There also would be no passing of the ball on offense and no forward laterals. Whichever team had accumulated the most points by the end of the second half would be declared the winner of the match.

"Pretty simple game, George," Dr. Herty said.

"Indeed!" George replied.

The two men shook hands again. They both wished each other good luck, turned and returned to their teams.

The time was now 3:30, and it was finally time for Auburn football to begin.

—25—

The good Colonel, along with his motley crew of Doc Greene and Buck, finally made it into the park. Doc and Buck quickly made their way down to where the Auburn team had gathered. An Atlanta police officer had accosted Buck and was unwilling to allow a Negro onto the sidelines. Doc intervened with a quickly concocted story that Buck was the API mascot, like the Georgia billy goat, and his presence on the sidelines was mandatory. The label of being a "mascot" infuriated Buck, but the bigoted officer got a sick laugh at the thought of Buck being compared to a goat and relented.

"Come on, Buck, let's go see history being made," Doc said and with that the two men joined the team.

Observing the battlefield upon arrival, Colonel Paul noticed a small ridge to the left and behind where the Auburn team would be standing. Ever the soldier, he decided this would be the best place for watching the game unfold. His thoughts were that perhaps he could spot something useful for George during the game and then communicate it to the Young Captain if he needed to make an adjustment. He also had no idea how the game would be played and wanted to be a safe distance away from any potential fights or melees. He was too old for that sort of thing now.

Colonel Paul arrived on his ridge just in time to observe George returning to his team from the meeting at the middle of the field. He had a glorious view of the entire park. The ridge was just high enough to see church steeples in a distant part of downtown Atlanta. The city had risen from Sherman's ashes.

Georgia would take the ball first. And what started in the first half was basically seventy minutes of punishing tackles, scrums, and pushing and shoving for both teams. The February cold and rain, along with the trampling from the men, had caused the dormant grass at Piedmont Park to become a quagmire. Colonel Paul watched in both admiration and astonishment as the two teams slugged it out like two armies pounding on each other at Antietam or Manassas. In his opinion, this was hand-to-hand combat. Something would have to give.

The Colonel was right. In the first half, the two teams had basically lined up and run the ball straight at each other, and neither team gave an inch. Because of the moisture and constant contact, the Auburn uniforms started appearing red while the Georgia uniforms took on an orange hue. The two teams were not only exchanging licks, they were exchanging colors from it.

The first half finally came to a merciful end. The score was 0 - 0. The refs stopped the game for a break, and both teams made their way off the field searching for relief. Colonel Paul picked his path off the ridge. He wanted to speak with George. Doc Greene and Buck helped administer what aid they could to the players on the sidelines. There were cuts, bruises, a few broken noses, some obvious sprains, and Doc was just thankful there were no broken bones protruding from any legs. From the sideline at field level, he got a very good look at the viciousness of the game. Never one to pass on a spirited drink, Doc was quickly sobered up by the brutality. He even told Buck at one point in the half it was "more like a brawl instead of a sport."

Colonel Paul made his way past the police officer who earlier had accosted Buck and headed onto the sidelines. The same officer gave the Colonel a cursory glance, but quickly decided he did not want any part of the old veteran. William made a straight line to George who had his back turned to him. The Young Captain was going over some notes he had made, both on the train and while the game was going on, while also keeping an eye on his battered team.

"George!" William said sternly.

Coach Petrie turned and was relieved to see his old friend walking toward him.

"Ah, Colonel Paul, fancy seeing you here." George replied.

To Colonel Paul's shock, the young captain was not rattled at all by the first half. He looked like he was comfortably in complete control of his emotions and the situation at hand. What a General he would have made, Colonel Paul thought.

Colonel Paul pointed toward his ridge and then spoke. "Now look, George, I have been watching the first half from that hill over there and I have some thoughts."

"It's a beautiful game, isn't it Colonel?" George said with a smile.

"I guess you could say that," the Colonel replied curtly.

"I know it can be a little harsh to the untrained eye the first time you see it," George said. "But there is a real rhythm to it."

"I will take your word on that. But from what I saw, we cannot continue to pound on each other all day."

George smiled. While going over his halftime notes, he had come to the same conclusion. He knew a breakout was needed. It took some study, but he finally found a solution.

"Manassas," George blurted.

"Manassas?"

"Yes, Manassas."

"Listen, Young Captain, I appreciate your love for all things historical especially a specific history that I am so acquainted with. But respectfully, just what in the hell does Manassas have to do with this current slugfest?"

Now George knew it was his time to shine. He knew in his heart that the falcon had finally become the falconer. He looked at the Colonel at that moment like the Colonel had looked at him so many times before. The tables had turned. George was the lecturer— the Colonel was the student.

"Colonel William Paul, my friend," George started, "what did General Lee do to General Pope at 2nd Manassas?"

At the same time, they said, "He hit him with a left hook."

There was a brief pause of silent admiration. Colonel Paul could see it now. Dr. Geroge Petrie had been setting this left hook up all during the first half. Auburn and Georgia were both equal in size, but Auburn did have one advantage in a giant of a man running the ball named Murphy. He was taller than the Colonel and easily weighed over two hundred pounds. The Colonel had watched during the first half as Murphy was handed the ball continually toward the right side of the Auburn line. Over time Georgia had deftly moved more and more defenders to that side of the field. Dr. Herty had been led to believe that this was the only side of the field that Auburn would run toward.

"Is there anything else?" George asked.

"No sir, that is all."

"Good, then. Enjoy the rest of the show, my friend."

Colonel Paul watched as George walked over to Doc, Buck, and his team. He saw George speak to Doc briefly. No doubt inquiring about the well-being of his players. The second half was almost set to begin. The team began to stir, loosen up a bit, and George pulled a few of his players aside. The Colonel turned and began to make his hike back to the small ridge where he observed the first half of the game. As he passed the police officer guarding a small gate, he muttered in amusement, "Manassas."

The police officer just shook his head in ignorance.

—26—

The second half of the game began with Auburn in possession of the football. It was almost a complete copy of the first half offensively for API. Murphy was handed the ball, he ran to the right side of the Georgia line, and he plowed into it for a gain of maybe one to two yards. A few times, the big man almost broke free, but Georgia had almost every player on their defensive team now focused on that side of the field. They stunted and crashed right on every play. At this point, the field, or what was left of it, was complete mud. The players' uniforms were so stained, you could barely tell the two teams apart during play.

Colonel Paul was back on his knoll in observation. He could see that the time was almost at hand for "Manassas." The Colonel was so focused on the game, he failed to notice that more and more people had gathered on the hill to watch. During halftime, hundreds of people had realized that it was the perfect place to watch the event.

Although the play was predictable, Auburn was having a little success bludgeoning Georgia. The offense moved the ball near midfield when on second down with two yards to go for new downs, Auburn gave the ball to Murphy again. Georgia was ready. The entire Georgia defense shifted pre-snap to their right side, and they stopped Murphy cold just one yard short of more downs. It was now third and one yard to go. George had a decision to make. His team could kick the ball, what was called a "punt," and relinquish control of the football to Georgia, or, they could run another offensive play and try to make the yard.

From the hill, Colonel Paul grinned knowing what was about to happen. He did not have to hear Dr. Petrie yell out "Manassas." He said to himself, *here we go.*

When Dr. Petrie said the word, Wright moved from his end position to the backfield next to Murphy. Georgia was not prepared for Auburn to go for the yard, and quickly moved from a punt receiving formation to their defensive one which strongly favored the right side of the Auburn line. The Georgia players were jumping up and down, moving more and more to that side of the field and were completely determined to stop Murphy from running for a new set of downs.

Quarterback Dorsey for Auburn took the snap like so many times before. He turned to hand the ball to Murphy like he had done almost every other play of the game. Young Wright moved to block in that direction to make a lane for Murphy to run through. The Georgia defenders pounced. Then, Dorsey jerked the ball suddenly away from Murphy. Wright stopped quickly and did an about face while Murphy moved in front of him without the ball. It was a perfect fake. Wright came behind quarterback Dorsey in full sprint moving parallel with the line of scrimmage. He had about a two-yard burst when Dorsey smoothly handed him the football. There were no Georgia defenders on that side of the field. It was completely empty.

From his vantage point, Colonel Paul saw it all unfold in a surreal slow motion. It was a wonderful maneuver, called just at the right time by a talented leader and executed perfectly by the players on short notice.

What the Colonel did not see was when Wright was handed the ball, he almost bobbled it. Because of the vast openness presented to him, he momentarily took his eye off the ball to look at the field. Luckily, he quickly regained full control of the ball, tucked it away beneath his left forearm and sprinted as fast as he could down the Georgia sideline past a shocked Dr. Herty. The Georgia coach was screaming and pointing at the ball carrier trying to get his defenders' attention as most of them tackled a now harmless Murphy.

George could see from his viewpoint that the play was a huge success. He also could see that one lone Georgia defensive man had seen the play unfold. That player was on the opposite side of the field and began at an angle to try and tackle Wright. It would be very close if he could catch the ball carrier.

The crowd was in full fury by now. The Auburn side cheering for the runner to cross the goal line and score while the Georgia side pleading for his apprehension. With an amazing effort, the Georgia player caught just enough of Wright's shoelace by diving to cause the Auburn back to stumble one yard short of scoring. A giant moan from both sides of the crowd was emitted.

Despite not scoring, "Manassas" had flipped the field clearly in Auburn's favor, and the Young Captain had his team just a few feet from scoring the first points of the game. The left hook had worked perfectly.

The very next play, George called for Dorsey to hand the ball off to Murphy again. Georgia was once again ready. They stuffed Murphy at the goal line not allowing him to score. Auburn huddled in between plays. Everyone in the park knew that the big back would be handed the ball again. But during the huddle, Murphy told Dorsey to keep the snap, lower his shoulder and he would come behind the quarterback to push him through the line for the score. On second down, with one yard to go, Dorsey took the snap. Just like Murphy said, he came behind the smaller Dorsey to push him through the line. But, at the last moment, he scooped the quarterback up and for all intents and purposes, threw him into the end zone over the line of scrimmage for a score. Touchdown, Auburn! The score of the game was API 4, Georgia State 0. In their first game ever, the men from the plains of East Alabama had taken the lead.

—27—

There was complete pandemonium after the first score of the game at Piedmont Park. The Auburn crowd yelled with excitement. A few students from API rushed the field to congratulate Dorsey and tried to carry him on their shoulders off the field. Colonel Paul thought he saw one of the women in attendance kiss Murphy. The Georgia billy goat escaped its handler, ran out onto the field and started bucking wildly with fear from the eruption of noise. One of the dignitaries travelling with the Mayor from the Auburn crowd could be heard above the roar shouting, "Shoot that damn goat!"

There was another level of excitement on the Georgia side. Dr. Herty for one was having a very heated discussion with one of the referees of the game. He was screaming about the rules of the game and that there were to be no forward passes today. Unfortunately they forgot to include any mention of throwing players in those rules. The Georgia crowd, by this point, was rabid. They had seen their team play football against Mercer University a few weeks before. This was the first time they had seen another team not only score on their boys but take a lead on them. To say they were irate would have been an understatement. And like George previously, Colonel Paul thought he could hear their fans making barking noises toward their players. He thought this was a strange way to motivate their players.

Through the brouhaha at the park, the Colonel noticed George on the sideline pacing, calm and completely focused on the task at hand. George motioned for his players to huddle in anticipation of the two-point play after the touchdown. The Auburn players broke their huddle and, like so many times before, tested the right side of the line with a hand off to Murphy. Like so many times before, the Georgia defense rallied and stopped the big back from gaining a yard. The Georgia boys held here just like Cobb's boys helped hold the stone wall at Fredericksburg. If they survived it, some of these boys today may have had uncles or fathers behind that wall in Virginia. Just like in 1863, nothing was coming through that line.

Colonel Paul could see the sun beginning to lower west of the park. It was getting late and so was the game. He understood that each half took seventy minutes to play. By his calculations, roughly fifty minutes had passed in the second half.

Georgia took back possession of the ball after the failed two point try by Auburn. The rabid Georgia crowd by now had whipped their players into a frenzy. In no time, the Georgia offense had moved the ball by dedicated running and solid blocking to about midfield. Colonel Paul could see that both teams had started to approach the point of exhaustion. It was exhausting for him just to watch.

Colonel Paul found the game riveting and he could not take his eyes off the action. He was now completely in tune with what was happening on the field. He had failed to notice a very special visitor who had joined the growing crowd on the hill watching the game. Only a few feet to his left was a young man with a large female golden eagle perched on his left arm. It was not until in between plays, when a very violent collision between two players had occurred, that the Colonel turned and saw the pair when the eagle's screech rose loudly above the crowd noise.

My God, a war eagle, the colonel said to himself. The old soldier and the bird locked eyes and stared at each other while the next few plays in the game unfolded. The handler of the bird caught the moment. The young man began to move closer to Colonel Paul with the bird.

"She fancies you, sir!" the younger man said to the Colonel.

"What is her name, son?"

"Her name is Saoirse."

"Saoirse, that is interesting. What does it mean?"

"It means freedom. It's an old Irish name for a free girl."

At this point there was a brief pause in the game. After a very physical run play, and even more violent tackle, the two teams began pushing and shoving one another near the Auburn thirty-yard line. It was late in the game and Georgia was moving the ball into Auburn territory. The team from Athens was desperate to tie the game.

Transfixed on the eagle, Colonel Paul spoke again. "An old Irish War Eagle."

"That's exactly what she is, sir," the man replied. "My father found her as a juvenile on a battlefield in the Wilderness in Virginia."

Colonel Paul turned pale. He took his eyes off the bird just long enough to get a good look at the young man holding her. The build was larger than his old friend's but there was no mistaking the resemblance in the face and eyes.

"Your father, was he a soldier?"

"Yes. Texas Brigade. Even fought with Hood and Longstreet. Was with them from Manassas through the Wilderness. His war ended when he was wounded at the Wilderness. But, not until he found this wounded girl lying next to him on the battlefield after the fight. They healed each other up," the young man stated proudly.

The Colonel asked the young man's name.

"James, sir. Paul James is my name."

"Your father, Alan, he survived the war?" the Colonel asked.

"Yes, sir. But how did you know his name, sir?"

"Because I am the man you are named after, son. I served with your father. I was good friends with him, and I have greatly missed him for many years now."

—28—

The field general knew it was getting late in the game. The sun was beginning to set on the far side of the field below the grandstands. Georgia had the ball and was moving deeper and deeper into Auburn territory. It would be up to his exhausted boys, clinging to a 4-0 lead, to stop the Georgians just a couple more times.

George believed in hard work. While preparing for this first game, he pushed his team to the limit physically. He knew it was for a moment just like this. The question now was did they know it? Knowing the work ethic, and the capabilities of the man coaching on the other sidelines, George was determined that his team would be more prepared than Georgia for this game. The young coach also had no choice. Georgia had already played and he had reluctantly been allowed a visit to see his opponent in person during their practice. He had left Athens, Georgia, not afraid, his spirit would never allow that, but more aware of the stamina required by his team to defeat such an experienced foe.

The Georgia quarterback would hand the ball off left. Then hand the ball off right. Then fake a hand off to the back and keep it himself. "First down!" the referee kept saying. Georgia was approaching the Auburn goal line. Somebody needed to make something happen and stop this momentum.

What would Longstreet do here? George questioned himself. *What would Lee do or Jackson, or Grant, or Sherman?* He started to focus in on these thoughts. Suddenly a loud pop and groan jostled him from his thoughts. On a second down play from the Auburn 22-yard line, a Georgia halfback was absolutely shattered by two Auburn defenders on a run play. George could not tell who the two players were that had made the vicious tackle. Play in the game stopped and several Georgia and Auburn players gathered around the hurt player on the field blocking the view from the sidelines.

One of the referees came over to inform Coach Petrie that there would be a minute delay in the game. The Georgia player, a young

Augustan, was not seriously injured but looked to be dazed. The referee also notified George that less than two minutes remained to be played in the match.

This pause gave George a few moments to gather his thoughts.

"We must attack," he decided. "We must stop this with some type of counter attack."

Only Buck heard George. The few players not in the game took water to the ones on the field. Doc Greene was also on the field attempting to aid the hurt Georgian with a few people from their staff.

Chamberlain, George thought to himself with a smile. His history studies brought him a northern solution, not a southern one.

He immediately headed onto the field and yelled for his team to gather around. The team quickly made their way to the coach and huddled around him. George could see how tired they were and that he had just one shot here to end the game.

"Chamberlain, men," he said.

No one responded.

"At Little Round Top, in Pennsylvania not too long ago, the Maine men led by their Colonel Chamberlain attacked with a swinging gate to stop the tide of rebels from swarming that hill!" he yelled. "He swept them down the hill and ended that part of the battle the second day at Gettysburg." Now George intended to do the same to the Georgia boys at Piedmont Park.

George proceeded to draw a small formation in the dirt for his team to study. He shifted three defenders further out to the left side of the defensive line than normal. One of the defenders was Wright, the small, quick back who had almost scored previously on Manassas. Next to him would be Dorsey, another quick back. Lupton and Murphy would be the hinge on the gate and bull rush the line. Hopefully, one of the two speedy backs could move around the bulge, and close the gate on the Georgia back. The right side of the defensive line would be vulnerable and would have to hold firm. When the huddle broke George grabbed Gaston and told him, "Not an inch on that side, never to yield!"

George made his way off the field with a confident stride. Doc Greene caught up to him just as both men cleared the sideline.

"How is the Georgia boy, Doc?"

"He will be fine. Probably a doozy of a headache tomorrow though."

"I know how he feels," George said just as he noticed something rising above the field.

—29—

The loud collision that startled George from his historical thoughts sent Sairose out of its keeper's arms and into the air. She did not fly much anymore, but the noise stirred something inside the old warbird. Paul James was not alarmed at all by her sudden departure. He and Colonel Paul first watched from the hill as she gloriously began to hover over the grandstand behind the Auburn sideline. In complete awe, the two men started moving down the hill toward the field as the golden eagle began to fly toward the middle of the field.

The referee that was about to restart the game, hesitated for a moment as the war eagle flew in circles from the middle of the field toward the Georgia side. She was stunning in that late afternoon sun. The light, glowing less and less by the minute, covered the bird with a golden aura. Time stopped as the entire crowd, including the players, stared at the creature. It was a sign.

George did not notice Colonel Paul on the sidelines. Like everyone else at the park, he saw the bird. It was now slowly flying in circles above the spot where he extended his defensive swing gate.

Colonel Paul then began to cheer. It was a low sound like a train in the distance gaining steam. A steady grumble at first. He began to yell, "*Warrrrrrrrrrrr.*"

George turned around. It was the first time since the halfway break of the game he had seen his old friend and he smiled with delight. The Colonel had taken off his hat, and had raised it high above his head while turning it in small circles and yelling something.

Buck then started in. Paul James joined, then Doc and the other Auburn players on the sideline. Instinctively, the Auburn crowd in the lower grandstand started the sound and motion, and then it spread all through the Auburn faithful.

"*Warrrrrrrrrrrr,*" drowned out the rabid Georgia fans barking mightily now at Sairose. She began to climb higher and higher. The noise was magnificent. George joined the cheer.

Just as the referee placed the ball back into play while signaling for the game to restart, the chant rose to a crescendo. Then, the Georgia quarterback took the snap, faked a hand-off to his left, turned right, and was blindsided by both Wright and Murphy. The ball was knocked loose.

"*Warrrrrrrrrrrr Eagle!*" The chant was finished.

"Ball, ball, ball," both sidelines screamed in agony. Lupton was there for Auburn.

The big man who had anchored both Auburn lines all day did more than just bullrush the right side of the Georgia line. He crushed it. The defensive lineman flattened two Georgia offensive lineman creating a hole that both Murphy and Wright rushed through. Taught to finish the drill, he followed the other two defenders into the backfield just in case another tackle had to be made. His efforts were rewarded with a fumble and about eighty yards of open field in front of him. Without hesitation, he picked up the football and rumbled down toward the Georgia goal line. George's swinging gate had worked!

From the sideline Colonel Paul looked on in complete and joyful disbelief. The Auburn side of the field erupted. An eerie silence fell over the Georgia side. Those dogs would not bark anymore this day.

Lupton was about to the Georgia thirty-yard line and gaining full steam before the players in red and black knew where the ball was. The only living thing near him was Sairose who had begun circling above the Georgia end zone. Lupton crossed the goal line, turned around to face midfield, and saw the entire Auburn team, coaches, and fans rushing toward him. With the football in one hand, and his other hand pointing at the bird in the air, he slammed the football down onto the ground. Auburn 8 - Georgia 0.

The referees rushed to that point in the field and began to clear out all non-essential people from the area. Men and women of all ages were there hugging players and screaming "War Eagle" as loud as they could. George had gotten caught up in the raw emotion of the play and was in the end zone hugging Buck. The mayor had fallen to the ground and was now covered in mud from head to toe. Tears streamed down his face. The game for all practical purposes was over, but the formality of the two-point conversion had to be finalized. Colonel Paul and his new friend Paul James seemed to be the only people who did not leave the sidelines. They offered each other cigars and began to enjoy the sweet flavor of victory. How sweet it was! Sairose remained in the air hovering over the crowd.

"Well, Colonel, Dad sure would have been proud of this spectacle today," the young man stated.

"No doubt, son. Somewhere in heaven he is smiling!"

George, along with some of the team members, and the entire Auburn faithful returned to their side of the field. The mayor was being helped off the field and all you could hear was him yelling to George, "You did it, Petrie! You really pulled this one off!"

By now the Georgia side had made its way down to their end zone. Dejected, they planned to make one final stand on the two-point conversion. This was to no avail. Broken and beaten, the Georgia boys could not stop Murphy running to the right one more time. Auburn 10 - Georgia 0. That was it. The referees called time and the game was over.

—30—

George made his way to midfield to congratulate Dr. Hearty from Georgia on a wonderfully played game. It was a proud moment and would always be a Saturday for him to remember. Walking to greet his friend, he could see the pain of the loss on the Georgia players' faces. He could not help but feel pity for them. *They really laid it on the line*, he thought. This would not be his last game for he had already agreed to coach three more. But before he greeted his friend, he had decided that those would be his last. He would go back to being just a general in the classroom.

"Dr. Hearty, that was a great game your boys played." Dr. Petrie spoke first.

"George, congratulations. You really mastered the field today," Dr. Hearty replied.

"Thank you for the match, sir. It was an honor."

"The honor is all mine, Dr. Petrie. See you again next year."

The two men embraced, then turned away from each other and returned to their respective teams. The Auburn side was elated. The Georgia side was in stunned silence.

For George, there was a feeling of relief more than anything. Quickly he made his way to his team. There would be no grand speeches, just hugs, smiles, and words of praise. "You did it!" was all he could say.

He let the boys know that they would not be travelling straight home to Auburn that evening. There would be a party for both teams tonight at Kimball House in celebration of the South's first football game. They all had one hour to clean up as best they could and then the team would travel to the hotel for the night's festivities. A victorious Auburn team roared in delight with news of this surprise.

As the team broke away, George began to search for his old friend Colonel Paul. He caught sight of him near the grandstands standing with a younger man now holding the mysterious War Eagle. He needed to talk to him.

Before he could get to the Colonel, the entire Auburn crowd surrounded George. Led by the mayor, the bankers along for the ride to watch their investment, and all the other dignitaries who travelled to Atlanta today, the crowd broke into cheers for Coach Petrie.

"Hip, hip, hoorah! Hip, hip, hoorah!" they chanted. George caught a glimpse of Colonel Paul and could see him laughing with approval. As the Young Captain wound his way through the crowd toward his friend, *For he's a jolly good fellow* broke out in unison. The practical, quiet young professor had won over Auburn and would now and forever be the toast of the town.

Taking a long pull from his cigar and then blowing out a mountain of smoke, Colonel Paul playfully said, "Well, Young Captain, I mean, Young General, Hood or Longstreet could not have managed it any better."

George extended his hand to shake the Colonel's and said. "You really think so, Colonel?"

Humble to the core, the Colonel thought, *this part of the country is sure lucky to have him.* "George, what I have witnessed here today—it will be history that will never be forgotten."

Bashfully, George shook the Colonel's hand and then pulled him in for a hug.

"War Eagle, Colonel!" George said.

"War Eagle, George!"

After the quick embrace, George turned to Paul James who had been standing there the entire time watching. "Now I want to meet that War Eagle," he said with a smile.

"Here she is, sir, her name is Sairose." Paul James walked over with her.

"Sairose . . . ah, she is free," George said while giving the eagle a soft stroke behind the head. The bird seemed completely at ease with the gentlemen.

"Yes, freedom. Other than my dad, you are the only other person I have ever met who knew the meaning of her name," he said.

George stared into the eagle's eyes for a moment. *What a beautiful creature,* he thought. *And, even better, good luck.*

"Well, gentlemen, will you please join us at Kimball House this evening?" George offered.

Colonel Paul answered first. "George, I have had enough of Atlanta today. I think Doc, Buck, and I are going to catch the 7:00 train back home."

Paul James also spoke, "Thank you, sir. This has all been an incredible experience today. I believe my bird here is ready to return home for rest also."

"Well, then, it was nice to meet you, and safe travels," George replied.

At that Paul James, holding Sairose, turned to Colonel Paul. A lively pro-Auburn crowd had grown near, and George could not hear what they said to each other. But both men had tears in their eyes and when they began to take leave of each other, Sairose let out a massive shriek.

The crowd carried George away from the Colonel. He tried to make his way back to him, but it was no use. As he grew farther and farther away from his friend, George waved goodbye. The Colonel waved back. George could not help but wonder if it might be one of the last times he ever saw him.

—31—

The Colonel waved goodbye to his friend George Petrie. With tears in his eyes, he said to himself, *Until we meet again.* He then turned and began to make his way from the field, through the grandstands and toward the train waiting for the departure back home. In the plaza leading toward the train station platform, he caught up with his other two friends, Buck and Doc Greene.

Joyfully he came up behind the two men, put one arm around each of them, and stated, "War Damn Eagle! How about those Auburn Tigers, men?"

The two men had huge smiles and repeated the sayings. They were happy to see that the Colonel would be travelling home to Auburn with them after the monumental victory today.

By the time the men arrived at the platform, the Colonel had finished his cigar. He carefully extinguished the butt on the bottom of his boot and discarded it in a garbage can near the train. In the can was another newspaper with an article about the game that would be happening today. The Colonel carefully picked the newspaper from the trash, folded it neatly and tucked it away into a pocket inside his leather duster. *History*, he thought.

The train porter yelled out, "All aboard," and the three Auburn men made their way to the back of the train to travel home.

Just before boarding the train, Buck stopped the men saying, "Look, you don't have to ride back here with me. There is plenty of room up front with the mayor and all the people going to the party at the Kimball House tonight."

Doc and Colonel Paul looked at each other and smiled to one another with understanding.

"Nonsense, Buck," Doc Greene said. "We all came up here together and we are damn sure all going back together."

"That's right," said Colonel Paul. "I would rather walk home then not ride next to you."

Buck nodded with appreciation and approval. He boarded first, followed by Doc Greene and the Colonel.

Colonel Paul stopped in the doorway of the train car and turned to take one more look at Atlanta.

"It is 1-1 now, Atlanta. This does not mean anything except that we are even," the old soldier said.

The three men took their seats as the train started moving slowly, then picked up steam and moved on down the line toward home.

Buck asked the men if they were hungry. He could go scrounge up some food or more brandy from the front if they liked.

Caught up in all the excitement, none of the three could recall the last time they had anything to eat. The rush of the game had suppressed their appetites.

"I would like some rum," Doc Greene said.

"Buck, I am fine. One thing though, could you fetch me some paper and a pencil if available?" the Colonel inquired.

"Yes, sir," Buck said. He could not help but notice that the Colonel looked like he was at peace.

Doc Greene and the Colonel sat quietly for a few moments. They stared out the windows both contemplating what they had witnessed.

Doc finally broke the silence, "I'm not sure I have the words to describe what I just saw."

"Me either, Doc. I think it will be up to George to carry that burden in remembering the story of today. He is the one that will have to tell the story so generations from now will know what happened."

"He is a good man," Doc Greene stated.

"Yes, the best Auburn man I know," the Colonel replied.

Buck made his way back to their car. He had found a little brandy for the men to share, some cold chicken, and another cigar for the Colonel. He also brought a piece of paper and a pencil.

The Colonel took the cigar and put it unlit into his mouth to chew on. He thanked Buck and took the pencil and paper.

Buck and Doc Greene shared the brandy and the chicken. They began to replay the entire game through their conversation. Both men could recall the game precisely and describe the match vividly. It was so natural for them it was like they had seen a hundred football games before. They both agreed to see many more games in the future.

The Colonel retreated into his thoughts. He took a deep breath, exhaled and said quietly, "This is for my friends back home." With that he put pencil to paper and began to write.

Who are these Texans,
Buried on the Auburn plains?
These 98 Gray Soldiers,
What are their names?

Why do I ask,
For their lost names?
Why do I care,
To know of their fames?

Where are they from,
And when did they fight?
Was I with them,
Did I share in their plight?

Did they come from Sabine,
Or were they born in Trinity?
Could some be from Galveston,
Tyler, Harrison, or Gillespie?

Did they see General Hood,
While fighting in the Devil's Den?
Did they charge with Longstreet,
As River of Death gunmen?

Could they speak of Cleburne,
The Irish Stonewall of the west?
Did they serve with Granbury,
A star of Waco's best?

Are they the 7th, 10th, 15th or 16th,
Or the 17th, 18th, 24th or 25th?
Is this the fearless Ross Cavalry,
Or the thunder of Hynson's battery?

In the fall will you Texans rest,
Or hear the Auburn cheers for our new game?
You Texans belong with us now,
And WAR EAGLE is your name.

Afterword

I consider myself one of the lucky ones who was born into the Auburn Family. My family uprooted from West Texas in 1974, and came to Auburn, Alabama. I was born, not long after the move, into a time before computers, cell phones, and in many places, cable television.

We spent a lot of time on beautiful Lake Martin in my youth. It was around those bonfires, on the front screened-in porches, and on long pontoon boat rides, that I listened to the many oral histories of friends and family members. Along with the stories of war, cars, farming, fighting, heartbreak, and true love, were many stories about Auburn Football. Those versions of history, that I still recall so vividly, were the inspiration for the story you have just read. It is my hope that it honors the people from my past who so deeply influenced the way I look at things, and how I communicate them.

Auburn is a special place and everyone has their own version of what it means to them. For me, the one thing I have always appreciated about it is the bond that it creates. There is a place at the table for everyone who chooses to become a part of the Auburn Family.

About the Author

Wade Bennett is a lifelong resident of Auburn, Alabama. He received his education there, beginning at Dean Road Elementary School, and finishing with a degree in Horticulture from Auburn University. He loves history, and has a special interest in the eastern theatre of the American Civil War, and the western theatre of World War II.

An avid golfer, he also enjoys pontoon boat rides on the lake, wiffle ball, cooking outside on the grill, and most of all, spending time with friends and family. He and his lovely wife, Valerie, have two wonderful boys, Paul and Jakeb John, who are the loves of their lives.